# OBSESSION

## ROYAL BLOOD BOOK ONE

ALEXIS CALDER

ILLARIA PUBLISHING

*For the girls who hide their dark side.*

Cover Artwork by Covers by Gillian
Editing by Court of Spice

# CHAPTER
# ONE

DANTE

THE BLADE BIT deeper into flesh and the shifter made a squeaking sound. My upper lip curled in disgust. This male was responsible for a trail of bodies, yet he shivered under my knife.

"Just tell me where you saw him last," I pressed. "You realize he'd give you over if it meant saving himself. Your loyalty is misplaced."

"You're wrong," the shifter hissed out through gritted teeth. "He saved my life."

I didn't hide my disdain. He clearly didn't know my brother well. He'd never purposefully do something kind. The misconception does explain why this one was harder to crack. Somehow, he truly felt loyalty. Most of the poor suckers my brother reigned in were just looking for their next fix. Which my brother was only too happy to provide. "He doesn't save lives. He takes them. You should know that better than most."

I'd been tracking my brother for a century already. Every time I got close, he'd vanish like smoke in the wind. The bodies were still fresh, so I knew I was close.

"We're setting things right. He told me you'd never understand," he said.

My temper flared, and I dragged the blade across his throat, cutting deep enough to go through tendons and muscle. Blood sprayed, coating my hands and forearms. I let the knife drop to the ground and the shifter's body slumped forward.

"He would have talked if you'd given him a few more minutes. I could feel his pulse racing. He was close," Anna said.

I glanced at my best friend. She was right, of course, but I had let the words get to me. "Bring in the other one."

She sighed. "You should wash off that blood."

Wolf shifter blood was toxic for vampires. At least that was what they said. But it had been decades since I'd felt so much as a sting from the stuff. "Bring him in."

"Whatever. Try not to kill this one before we get the information we need." She lifted her brows and gave me a stern expression before walking to the door.

Anna was the only person in the world I'd let speak to me that way. She'd earned that right and she knew it.

A moment later, a figure with a black bag over his head was shoved into the room. He stumbled forward, stopping inches from the pooling crimson spilling out from his dead friend.

Anna kicked him in the back of the knees. He groaned as he fell, landing hard on the cement floor. With a whimper, he steadied himself and turned his head from side to side, as if he'd be able to see through the fabric covering him.

"You can smell the blood, can't you?" I asked.

"Such a waste, isn't it?" Anna purred. "Killed before I got a sip. But you smell delicious."

The front of his pants grew wet and I my nose wrinkled. Pathetic. Why hadn't we started with this one?

"Did he piss himself?" Anna hissed.

"Yeah," I said. "Real tough guy we have here."

"Killing humans is fine, but when the tables are turned, you can't handle the heat, can you, asshole?" Anna slammed her foot into his back, knocking him down so he landed face-first in the warm, wet blood.

He pressed himself up, his hands making squelching sounds as he pulled them away from the ground. "Don't kill me. Please, don't kill me. I'm human. I'm not like the rest of them."

I glanced at Anna, and she just shook her head. It was rare we got a human who was aware of our world, but it happened sometimes. It didn't change this man's fate, though. He'd made his choice.

Anyone working with my brother was living on borrowed time. Even if they didn't know it yet. I'd hunt each and every one of them down until I killed them all.

They called me a monster, but I was nothing compared to my brother and his henchmen. "Where's Vincent?"

"I don't know any Vincent," he said.

"Take off his hood," I commanded.

Anna tugged it off and I crouched in front of him, my elbows resting on my thighs, a clean knife in my hand. I held the hilt with the blade pointing up. "Where is he?"

"I swear to you, I don't know anyone named Vincent." He was sweating and his eyes bulged with fear.

"Where's your boss?" Anna asked.

"Probably at home with his wife and kids," he said. "What you want with Charlie?"

I rose, then tilted my head to the side, making my neck crack. This man was either incredibly stupid or he was better than I initially thought. Considering the fact that he wet himself, I was betting on the former.

With careful steps so I didn't get too much blood on my shoes, I approached the fallen body. Gripping the dead male's hair, I lifted the face from the floor so our guest could see exactly where his boss was. "Charlie made his choice. Now, it's time for you to show me exactly why you shouldn't join him."

The man panted and his eyes bulged even wider. "That's my boss. That's Charlie. I worked for him. That was it. He was all I knew. I never saw no one else."

"Where do the drugs come from?" Anna's words were tight, and I knew she was losing her patience nearly as much as I was.

"What drugs?" he asked.

"Don't tell me you thought your boss was on the level?" I released my grip on Charlie and his head hit the cement with a crack.

The other man winced and turned away from the body. "I know about the drugs. Someone drops off the shipment every week at the liquor store. Packed in boxes the same as the booze. Only it ain't booze." His words tumbled out between panting breaths. "But there're different suppliers."

Of course. They weren't just running lotus; they were running all the traditional human drugs, too. I glared at Charlie on the ground. Based on the bruises adorning his wife when I stopped by to retrieve him, I was guessing there weren't going to be a whole lot of people who mourned his passing. She'd stood silently by while I hauled him away.

"The lotus," I said. "Who brings it in?"

He's shaking and holding his hands in front of me, fingers splayed open as if in surrender. "I don't know."

I growled and took a step toward him. He was no use to me if he couldn't give me any information.

"But I saw where it came from!" he shouted, desperation making his voice high pitched.

I froze and gave him a nod of encouragement. "Go on."

"Some place called Lost Harbor. It was on the address labels. That's all I know," he said.

"Dante..." Anna's tone was a warning, but I wasn't listening anymore. Of all the places to follow this lead, Lost Harbor is the last one I wanted to visit.

"Fuck," I breathed out.

"Why would he go back home?" she asked. "That doesn't make sense."

"It doesn't matter." I glanced at the human. "You did good."

"So I can go? I can leave?" He was still sweating and I could smell the fear mingling with the fast food he'd eaten earlier today. My stomach churned. I hadn't fed in days, but I wasn't about to eat him. I had standards.

I looked at Anna. "He's all yours."

She grinned and a delighted gleam flickered in her eyes. Her fangs extended. She'd never been picky about her food.

As I walked out of the room, I heard a sharp cry of pain, then silence.

# CHAPTER
# TWO

Isla

TODAY WAS ten years to the day since I was sold to the Crescent Pack. Ten years since my own mother signed the paperwork in blood, giving her one and only child to a ruthless alpha and his cronies to do with as they wished.

I suppose I should be grateful. Some of the girls here were sold to the pack when they were much younger. I was thirteen when my mom couldn't afford to take care of me anymore. I tasted freedom longer than most humans around here.

My path was different in a lot of ways. Most of the other human women served as entertainment, rather than getting into official pack business. They were obedient and eager to serve. Hoping that one of the males would take them as a mate and raise their status.

That wasn't me. I was mouthy and sarcastic; never obedient. Even after daily beatings when I first arrived, I didn't learn my lesson. But the pack hadn't purchased me for my appearance. It wasn't that I was ugly, I was pretty enough, but I never played up my looks. That wasn't my lot in life. I was going to get the fuck out of here, not end up trapped like my mom.

Growing up with a mom who made a living on her back taught me that looks fade. The older she got, the more she struggled to pay her bills. As she aged, her clients changed. They were less important, less attractive, and less wealthy.

So we had less.

I refused to be like her.

Sure, I liked sex as much as the next girl. But when I fucked, it was for me. Not for them. I wasn't against my mother's profession; but I wanted a different path. I wanted to get the fuck out of here. Live in a human city, away from the monsters. Where people like me, people without magic, could blend in and live without fear.

Which is how I found myself here, crunching numbers and working on payroll for the Crescent Pack's many businesses. Most of them illegal. It was my job to make them look legal enough to keep the Supernatural Council out of their business.

Ten fucking years.

But only a few more months until I reached my goal. I'd have enough for the bribes to pay for transport out, in addition to a good chunk to help me find a new place outside the magical wards of Lost Harbor.

A knock on the door shook me from my thoughts and I jumped from my chair, expecting to see my boss.

When Ryder walked in, I slouched back against my seat. "What do you want?"

Ryder was the alpha's son. He was six-three of chiseled muscle and hard edges. His midnight colored hair always looked like he'd just had sex, and his green eyes could pierce your very soul. Perpetual dark stubble covered his strong jaw, making his perfectly soft lips stand out even more.

Every woman wanted Ryder; shifter and human alike. Which is part of why most of the women here hated me. Because for two years, he'd been mine. Now, he was a pain in my ass.

"Is that any way to greet your future alpha?" he asked.

I quirked a brow. "I'm not a shifter, so you're not my alpha."

"You're pack property," he reminded me. "Even more reason for you to show respect."

"I might be pack property on paper, but you know better than anyone that I make my own rules," I said.

"You're going to get yourself killed with your insolence one of these days, Isla," he said.

"Good thing that's no longer your problem," I said.

"This is why we're not together anymore. You just don't know when to keep your mouth shut," he said.

"I thought you liked it when I opened wide." I formed

my mouth into the shape of a large O, then closed it slowly.

"If you're offering…"

"I'd rather blow a vampire than go down on you," I said.

"Still so bitter," he said.

"You fucked six girls on the same night and expected me to be cool with it." Most shifters had trouble with loyalty unless they found their true mate. It was one thing to have the occasional fling, it was completely different to attend an orgy the same night you tell a girl you want to marry her.

"Maybe you shouldn't have turned my proposal down," he said.

Okay, so some of that was on me. I might have loved him once, but even he wasn't enough to get me to stay. In a million years, I never thought he'd propose. Our relationship was fun, and we were good together until we weren't. I couldn't be his partner in the way he needed me to. I couldn't be his arm-candy at pack events. Mindlessly smiling and taking orders wasn't something I was capable of.

To be fair, I didn't break up with him after he proposed. I just told him I didn't want to marry him. After the six girl orgy? That's when I dumped his ass.

"Why are you here, Ryder?" I asked.

"I wanted to see if you had a date for tonight," he said.

"You know I don't," I replied. After getting involved with him, I learned my lesson. No more relationships.

Nothing that might prevent me from reaching my goal. I didn't want to be tied to Lost Harbor when there was a whole world waiting for me to explore.

"Maybe you'd want to go as friends?" he asked.

My brow furrowed. "Can we even be friends?"

He shrugged. "I miss you."

"You miss me?" I was skeptical. He had a new girl every night. I knew because most of them went out of their way to tell me they'd been with him. As if I was supposed to explode into a jealous rage or something.

There was so much fucking drama in this pack.

Oddly, it never bothered me. Another reason I knew I shouldn't marry him. Call me a hopeless romantic, but it seemed like you should care about your lover fucking someone else if you were meant to be together.

"I miss your pussy," he said.

"Oh, there it is." Even as I tried to play it off as nothing, tension coiled low in my belly. I hadn't been with anyone since the breakup and the toys weren't cutting it anymore. Six months was a long drought.

As much as I didn't want to go back to being with Ryder, I had to admit he was quite skilled in the sex department.

I squeezed my legs together. The last thing I needed was for him to smell my arousal. *Down girl.* Stupid shifters and their stupid good senses.

"Come on, it wasn't all bad. Even you have to admit that the sex was spectacular. I get that you want your freedom, but it doesn't mean we can't enjoy each other's company," he said. "I know you're not fucking anyone else."

"Keeping tabs on me?" I asked.

"I'll be alpha next year. I have to keep tabs on everyone," he said.

"Just ask one of your groupies," I said.

"Since my dad announced his retirement date, they've been non-stop. They all come with strings attached. Me and you, we could be about fucking. We were always good at that," he said. "I already know you don't want to marry me."

"Ryder..." He was making me feel guilty. But there were dozens of girls who would happily pop out a whole litter of shifter babies for him.

"All I'm asking is that you consider it," he said. "No pressure."

"I'll think about," I said.

He grinned. "I'll be wearing a devil mask at the party. Find me."

"How appropriate and unoriginal," I said.

"I knew you'd say that."

"Won't your other admirers miss you if you sneak off with me?" I asked.

"You jealous?"

"Do I look jealous?"

He dragged his tongue across his lower lip and raked his eyes up and down my body. I couldn't smell arousal the way shifters could, but I didn't need the extra senses to know what he was thinking.

An involuntary shiver ran down my spine, and my traitorous vagina responded to his words. *Dammit.* He was going to know how wet I was already just thinking about us together.

It had been so long since I'd been with anyone. Too long.

"I'll see you tonight," he said, his eyes dipping down as if he could see my pussy through the desk and my clothes.

"This doesn't mean we're a couple," I warned.

"I don't need a relationship to worship your body," he said.

*Holy fuck*, I was in trouble.

"Don't bother wearing panties." He left the office, closing the door behind him.

# CHAPTER
# THREE

Isla

ANGELS AND DEMONS night was the most popular holiday in Lost Hollow. Parties happened all over town and every business closed for the night. Of course, no actual angels or demons were present. Nobody had seen those creatures in centuries. But that didn't stop the shifter packs from mingling for a night of debauchery.

While the shifters didn't cross into vampire, witch, or fae territory, they were free to mix and mingle among the various shifter sub-species. With the masks everyone wore, the only way you'd know which kind of shifter you were with was by scent. For us few humans who lived in the packs, it would remain a mystery. Some of the girls I grew up with looked forward to this night all year, hoping to score a tumble with a shifter they'd never tried.

Typically, I wasn't out for a hook-up. But then again, I'd been dating the future alpha for the last two years. My evening entertainment had been guaranteed.

Maybe it was again this year.

If I was willing to fall back into old habits with Ryder.

It was a tempting proposition. He already knew every curve, every scar, every freckle. Ryder knew exactly where to touch and how much pressure to use. It would be so easy; so safe. We'd both get an orgasm and then we could move on.

But I knew that everything came at a price. There were no favors in the Crescent Pack. Even if it sounded like it was tit for tat, fucking Ryder would have strings.

I could almost feel his calloused hands sliding down my hips, his nimble fingers dipping inside. My clit throbbed in anticipation. There was only so much a girl could take care of herself.

Maybe I didn't care that this would cost me later. Maybe one night to release some of this pressure would be worth it. I could risk finding another male. That wouldn't be an issue. There was always someone in the mood. Just yesterday I'd walked past Dominick pounding away at some random human in the middle of the hallway. Lack of options wasn't my issue.

My problem was that I'd seen how needy even the most stoic male shifters could get. Once they had you, they thought it was an open invitation any time they wanted. I wasn't looking for a partner or even a fuck buddy. I didn't want the distractions.

I wanted Ryder. At least for tonight.

Determined to take him up on his offer, I unzipped the ballroom gown I'd selected for the party and tossed it on the bed. If I was going to take Ryder into my bed tonight, I was going to spend the whole night getting him warmed up.

The sleek, silky black dress hanging in the back of my closet had never been worn. Between the plunging neckline, high slit on the side, and curve hugging fabric, it left nothing to the imagination. This dress was a weapon. And I intended to wield it against a certain future alpha tonight.

I looked myself over in the mirror, touching up the fire-engine red lipstick one last time. The hazel eyes staring back at me were identical to my mother's. I'd learned how to use makeup from her. While I didn't wear it often, I supposed I should thank her for teaching me how to use it properly. It felt like a mask, or war paint. Something I put on when I needed a shield between myself and everyone around me. It kept people from seeing too much of who I really was.

Those two years I'd been with Ryder, I wore a lot of makeup. It had only been recently that I'd let myself tone it down, sometimes even skipping it altogether.

Blowing out a long breath, I gently combed my fingers through my long brown hair, breaking up some of the tighter curls from the curling iron. I smoothed out the fabric of the dress. It hugged my curves in all the right places.

I grabbed the half-mask off the counter. It was the same white feathered mask I'd worn every year. A contrast to the red devil Ryder always wore.

Of all the parties and events hosted on angels and demons night, the hottest ticket in town was the Crescent Pack's masquerade ball. Only the pack's inner circle and their dates would be permitted entrance. I'd started attending a year before Ryder and I got together.

The alpha knew I was valuable, and he'd rewarded my hard work with that elevation in my status. It was where I'd first noticed Ryder. Sure, I'd seen him around, but I'd never really *seen* him. We started dating shortly after the party. I shook away the nostalgia. Memories had a way of showing the world through rose-colored glasses. I couldn't afford to make that mistake.

I walked out of my room into the living room I shared with my roommate, Maddie. She was sprawled out on the couch in her sweatpants, hot pink hair in a messy bun, her arm stuffed inside a bag of Cheetos. Her eyes widened when she saw me and she dropped the bag. "Holy shit, you tore the tags off. Who's the mark?"

I shrugged, then walked to the kitchen counter and poured myself a bourbon. "Nobody special."

"Liar," she said. "You don't wear that dress unless you want to own a man's balls for the night."

I tossed back the drink in one swallow, then slammed the glass on the counter before turning to her. "Why aren't you dressed? You have to have at least a few party invitations for tonight."

She cocked a brow. "You think I'd be caught dead dolled up at one of those events?" She shuddered. "I don't need a bunch of drunk and horny males pawing all over me all night."

I made a sound that was supposed to be agreement, but came out sounding a lot more like a guilty squeak.

She laughed. "Girl, you get it. Just keep it down if you bring him back here. I'm going to bed early so I can sleep through the part of the night where I question all my life choices and drunk call my ex."

Hand on my hip, I scolded her, "You know you can do better. Everyone knows you can do better."

She grabbed a Twizzler from the package on the table and took a bite. "I don't want to do better."

Maybe something was wrong with me. Maybe my heart was made of stone, as Ryder had accused me after we broke up. When we were done, I just moved on. Not with another lover, but with my life. No tears, no heartache. Things didn't feel much different than they had when we'd been together. There weren't a lot of highs and lows in my life. I mostly just existed. Trying to get from one day to the next.

Okay, so maybe I was broken, and Maddie's reaction to her girlfriend of a year breaking up with her was far more normal.

I walked over to my friend and kissed her on the head. "Don't do anything stupid. I'll be back later."

"Don't worry about me. Just give me all the details so I

can live vicariously through you when you get back," she said.

"You don't even like dick," I said.

"I still appreciate a good orgasm story." She bit into the Twizzler.

"You sure you don't want to come?" I asked. Maddie was a shifter and her father had rank in the pack. She could be part of all the drama if she wanted. Instead, she chose to downplay her status and only joined in pack events when required.

"Fuck no." She grabbed the fallen bag of Cheetos. "I'm good right here."

I grabbed my leather jacket and slipped it over my shoulders. "Alright. I'll see you later."

Maddie wouldn't want me to stay and wallow with her. Besides, there was a very good chance she and Kaylie would be back together by next week. It wasn't the first time they'd broken up. Kaylie wasn't who I'd want to spend the rest of my life with, but the two of them had undeniable chemistry, and when things were good, they were *good*. But they both had typical shifter tempers, and when things were bad, they were nuclear.

Every break up gutted her. Then she was willing to go through it all over again at the chance that maybe it would be different. I zipped up my jacket as I stepped out into the cold evening air. Love was poisonous; it was a drug. It destroyed who you were and turned you into something you didn't recognize. You lost part of yourself when you started living for someone else. If the poison didn't kill you, the withdrawals when it was over would.

It was better to be alone.

CHAPTER
# FOUR

Isla

FASHIONABLY LATE ISN'T REALLY a thing at a shifter party, but I tried to arrive well after things were in swing. Most of the guests were already at the sprawling mansion that over-looked the lake.

Purple and blue lights glowed along the white stone building and lit up the cement walkways. Through the dozens of massive widows, I could see flickering lights in a rainbow of colors. The valet hadn't batted an eye when he took my keys, but the shifters lingering on the front porch didn't hide their inspection.

They hadn't even seen the dress yet.

The bass hit me before I opened the door, making my bones vibrate. When Sarah, the alpha's current favorite human, opened the door, the music nearly swallowed me whole.

"Can I take your coat?" Sarah yelled over the din.

I handed it to her. I guess she wasn't the favorite anymore. Not if she was working the coat room.

"Enjoy the party," Sarah said.

I narrowed my eyes briefly, trying to detect the sarcasm in her tone. She smiled. A pretty, vapid expression. She was genuine.

She was exactly why I couldn't be with any of the members of this pack. That's what they expected from females. Especially humans. I offered a forced smile before heading into the crowd.

I rarely dressed up, but I knew I killed it in this dress. Most of the males moved out of my way, keeping their distance from the future alpha's former girl. But a few of them were more daring, watching me with hungry expressions. There was power in the way I looked tonight. A woman owning her sexuality. It sent a delicious little thrill down my spine. I wasn't used to being an object of desire. Before Ryder, I actively avoided it. While I was with him, I was his. Nobody looked at me in a way that might piss him off. Tonight, I was taking that back. And it felt good.

"Isla, hey." Derek Jones, one of the alpha's closest friends, grabbed my elbow. His dark eyes flicked up and down, not even hiding the fact that he was taking in every inch of my curves. He smirked. "You clean up nice."

He was a handsome male. His silver hair cut a striking contrast against his brown skin. And he looked amazing in a suit. The problem was, he was old enough to be my father, and I just wasn't into that. But Derek wasn't someone you disrespected. "Kind of you to notice."

"If you dressed like this more often, I'd have noticed sooner," he said.

Internally, I cringed. "I don't attend many parties."

"That's a damn shame. I think you should attend more." He dragged his fingertip up my bare arm. "Tell me, did you attend this event alone tonight or is there another male I need to challenge for your attention?"

Before I could open my mouth, another hand gripped my opposite arm. "She's with me."

Derek dropped his hand. "My apologies, Ryder. I didn't realize you two had patched things up."

Ryder made a possessive sound like a low growl, and Derek walked away without another word.

Eyebrow raised, I spun to face Ryder. He was wearing a black tuxedo and his red devil mask. I'd forgotten just how good he looked in a tux. It took me a moment to collect my thoughts, but I shook the fog of lust from my mind. "We're not together. You didn't have to do that."

He lifted his hands in the air. "I guess I interpreted the cry for help in your expression wrong. If you want to go after him, by all means, don't let me stop you. I didn't know you had a daddy kink."

"Maybe I do. Maybe I will fuck someone else tonight. It doesn't have to be you. I'm sure Derek has plenty of experience," I said.

He laughed. "You're practically a born again virgin since we broke up. I know you haven't been with anyone."

"You don't know everything about me," I said.

"I know Derek is about the only one ballsy enough to shoot his shot with my ex," he said. "Only because he knows my dad needs him around."

I never knew exactly what Derek's skill set was, but he was second only to the beta. He was practically pack royalty.

Ryder slid a possessive arm around my waist as his eyes raked up and down my body. A low growl sounded in his throat, and I could see the hungry look in his expression. "Don't tell me you didn't wear this dress just for me. I know you, Isla. This dress was intentional. And not for scoping out some random male."

He was correct, of course, but I couldn't let him know that. "I have options. What are you going to do to keep me from running off to someone else? Maybe I'm into the older ones," I said.

It was a game between us tonight. I was still comfortable enough around him to trust him. Like every wolf shifter, Ryder had a dangerous temper. I'd seen it come out more than once, but never at me. He was different with me than he was with the rest of his pack. Maybe that was part of why I couldn't love him the way he needed me to. I could love the Ryder I saw when we were alone, but his alpha side was reckless and dangerous. When it came to his pack, it was all-consuming. Pack was everything, and I wasn't a shifter. I knew it if came down to it, he'd choose his pack over me every single time.

Ryder's hand slid over the silky fabric of my dress, starting low at my hip and working its way up toward my breast. His hand lingered high enough that his thumb skimmed the underside of my breast. "No bra." Ryder's eyes flashed with wicked glee and my face flushed.

I'd come here tonight with the expectation that Ryder would slip this dress off of me. But I couldn't make it too easy for him. "Are you going to ask me to dance, or should I find someone else?"

He dropped his hand from my side, then offered his elbow as if he were an actual gentleman. He could play the part, but I knew what lurked beneath. Over the last few months, I'd had more glimpses of his power taking hold. He knew how to give orders and how to command. He'd never been like that with me, and part of me wanted to know what that was like.

We lost ourselves in the music, laughing and talking like old times. I couldn't believe how easily we'd fallen back into those familiar roles. It was too easy, too comfortable. This was supposed to be a hookup, not a reconciliation.

The music slowed, and the couples around us on the dance floor got closer, more intimate. Ryder pulled me in until I was pressed flat against him. His lips brushed against my ear, his breath warm against my skin. We moved to the music and his mouth moved lower until he reached my jaw. He kissed me softly, moving lower until his tongue flicked out against my neck. Shivers ran down my spine and I practically moaned as the heat began to build. I could feel the curve of his smile against my jaw before he whispered, "I forgot just how good you taste. Do you still taste as sweet between your legs?"

His teeth nipped at my ear and I had to press my lips together to keep from making a primal sound.

I let my fingers wander, sliding them up the crisp white shirt and feeling his firm muscles underneath. "Do you still say my name when you're with others?" I asked.

"Darla has a big mouth." He tried to scowl, but I could see the laughter in his eyes.

"You know this changes nothing between us," I said.

His hand moved to the slit of my dress and his fingers brushed against the bare skin of my exposed thigh. His hand rose beyond the slit and he was able to tell that I indeed had done as requested and skipped the undergarments altogether.

He groaned into my ear. "You naughty girl."

His hardness pressed against my hip, and I wanted nothing more than to grind my body into his. If we did it right here on the dance floor, nobody would care. It wouldn't be the first time a couple had lost their inhibitions at one of the alpha's parties. But we weren't a couple, and being human meant I had an innate urge for discretion. Something that shifters didn't seem to possess.

I rose on my toes and guided his head down enough so I could whisper to him. "Should we find somewhere a little more private? Or we could go to my place."

Ryder didn't need to be asked twice. He clasped my hand and led us off the dance floor. My heart thundered in anticipation. I needed this; I needed the release. For the last several months, all I had done was go through the motions. I did my job, read books, went for runs, and I hung out with Maddie. But it felt a little too empty. I needed that reminder that I was still alive. Sex with Ryder was exactly the boost I needed.

# CHAPTER
# FIVE

Isla

RYDER LED me away from the pounding bass, back toward the entrance. I thought we'd take the stairs to one of the many bedrooms, but we headed toward the front door instead. We'd never had sex outside before. Flutters of anticipation filled my chest at the thought.

We neared Sarah, who was manning the table in front of the oversized coat closet. I scowled. "I'm not open to a third tonight, Ryder."

He chuckled. "Oh, I remember the one time we tried that. You were so possessive of me I thought you might actually be a wolf shifter under that human facade."

"Don't make me bite you," I warned.

"Promises," he said.

Ryder stopped in front of Sarah and fixed a Cheshire

grin on his lips. "Sarah, darling, I need you to step away from the closet for a while."

She leaned down so her cleavage was on full display. "What did you have in mind?"

"Go get a snack or dance with someone. Just leave the closet for about twenty..." Ryder glanced at me, "Make that forty minutes."

I cocked a brow. "Someone thinks highly of himself."

He ignored me and kept his attention on Sarah. "Nobody needs anything from you for a while. Go on."

She pouted, sticking her lower lip out. I rolled my eyes, though it didn't do a whole lot of good. She'd kept her gaze locked on Ryder from the moment we arrived.

"I'm sure that's not true, Ry," she said. "I know I could be of service to you."

"Go, now." It was a command. His tone was confident and calm, but there was an edge to it, a touch of power that he rarely used.

It sent a shiver straight to my core.

Sarah whined, but she left without a single glance at me.

"Now, where were we?" Ryder turned his attention to me, his voice already husky with lust.

"I believe you promised me forty minutes," I said.

He tugged me past the desk into the waiting coat room. It was a huge space, the size of a master bedroom. The scent of leather mingled with smoke and gasoline. The smell of the Crescent Pack clinging to the leather jackets hanging on sturdy racks that protruded from each wall.

Ryder released my hand. "The bedrooms are probably full and I wanted someplace new."

That was a challenge. We'd probably had sex in every room in this house. Except this one. Maybe he was taking this seriously as a hookup and not a chance that we were getting back together. There was something about a closet that felt less intimate than the other places we'd been.

"It's different." I was still taking in the surroundings when the light went out. I yelped, then felt Ryder's hands on my body. "Shhh, just go with it. Let me enjoy your body. Let me worship you."

How was I supposed to argue with that?

Ryder pushed me against the wall, shoving the coats aside. His mouth was on me in a heartbeat; kissing my neck as his hands slipped under the thin fabric of my dress.

I leaned back against the wall, closing my eyes. Ryder's hands moved up toward my aching breasts. I moaned as Ryder's hands caressed them, creating a barrier between my peaked nipples and the fabric. When he dropped his hands, I grunted in protest. The dress felt harsh against my sensitive flesh and I needed it off.

As if he could read my thoughts, Ryder gathered the fabric in his hands and lifted it over my head. His hands cupped my face, and he pressed against me as his mouth claimed mine. The kiss was angry and intense, as if he was releasing all of the tension between us the last few

30

months. My lips parted and his tongue slid in, meeting mine in wild thrusts.

Moaning into the kiss, I ground against his hardness, eager to feel him inside me. It had been too long, and I'd deal with whatever the aftermath was just for that sense of release.

Without breaking the kiss, I started to work the buttons on his shirt before moving to his jeans. He smiled against my mouth and a rush of heat surged, making me even wetter. I reached down and got my hand on his cock for a moment before he caught my wrist and lifted it away. "Naughty, impatient girl."

"Stop teasing," I said, nearly breathless.

"I told you, I'm going to enjoy you for a while." He pulled away. I could only make out the shadow of his form in the darkness, but I swore I could feel the heat radiating from him. He wanted this just as much as I did. Maybe even more.

With shifter speed, he grabbed my other wrist and lifted my hands until they were pinned against the wall above my head. He dropped one hand, gripping both of my wrists securely with one of his large hands.

I swallowed hard, my heart racing. When we'd been together, sex had been good, but it had been safe and predictable. The craziest thing we did was choose different locations. This was new. Different. I bit down on my lower lip, enjoying the direction he was going.

Suddenly, I felt something tight on my wrists, binding them together. I gasped. "What are you doing?"

"Making sure you can't run off on me while I make you scream my name," he said.

My breath caught in my throat and I tensed as he tightened what I think was his belt around me. He tied it to the rod that held the coats and as soon as he removed his hands, I tugged, testing. It held fast. I pulled harder and a little rush of panic surged. I wasn't going to be able to get out of this on my own. "Ryder..." I wasn't sure if I liked this as much anymore.

He silenced me with his mouth, kissing with intensity and fire. The fear I'd felt melted away, and I leaned forward, wishing I could run my fingers over his bare chest. I wanted to touch every inch of him now that I couldn't, and it was driving me insane.

Ryder broke the kiss, then grabbed my chin, a little harder than I expected. It sent a thrill that shot right to my core. Why did I like this so much?

His other hand slid down my body, passing my breasts until he reached my pussy. Clamping a hand around it, he leaned in to me, "This is mine."

My eyes widened, and my heart raced.

"Tell me, tell me who this belongs to," he rasped.

I sucked in a breath. This was just sex, it was make believe. And it was making me soaking wet.

He slapped my pussy, making me wince from the sting. "Tell me, Isla."

"It's yours," I hissed, startled, and a little surprised at how turned on I was.

"That's what I thought." He shoved two fingers inside me, and my back arched, grinding into his thrusts.

He curved his fingers, hitting me in just the right place as he thrust in and out. A moment later, his mouth was on the bundle of nerves at my apex. His tongue adding to my pleasure, making stars dance in my vision as pressure coiled. The sensations built and my moans grew louder with each thrust.

His thumb rubbed against the sensitive nub, pushing me into another climax. Waves of pleasure rolled through me, nearly breaking me. I writhed under his touch and tension built low in my belly.

Ryder stood, continuing to work his fingers. His hot breath was against my neck and his mouth found my earlobe. "That's a good girl," he whispered into my ear. "Come for me."

And I did.

When he removed his hand, I let out a breath of relief. I needed the time to catch my breath. "Holy shit, Ryder." This was different from what we'd done in the past. "You've been holding out on me."

"I learned some new tricks while we were apart." He pressed against me, and I could feel his hardness digging into my side. He'd ditched the pants, and I was so ready to feel that impressive length inside me.

I didn't even care who he'd been with to improve his game. I just needed him. Without thinking, I reached for him, but my bindings held. A whine escaped my throat. The sound surprised me, but Ryder seemed to like it. He growled, a feral, possessive sound that made my toes curl. "Beg for me."

"Please." I wasn't even thinking anymore. My mind was too foggy with lust. I didn't care how I behaved, I didn't care that he was making me beg. "Please."

He leaned in, his lips near my ear, "Please what?"

"Please fuck me," I managed. If I didn't get him inside me, I was going to explode.

Ryder grabbed my breasts, his calloused hands rough and greedy. I moaned my approval.

Suddenly, light sliced through the darkness.

"Whoa, sorry, man."

I yelped. "Get out!"

"Sorry, Ryder, we need your help with something."

I growled, making a sound I didn't even know I was capable of making. "Not a good time, Jake." I didn't care if Jake was Ryder's second. I didn't care that I was naked. I wanted him to close that door and let us finish this.

"Can this wait?" Ryder said through gritted teeth. His hands were still gripping my breasts.

"We've got trouble. Your dad asked me to get you. It's bad," Jake said.

"Fuck." Ryder released my breasts and ran a hand through his hair.

I was going to have the worst case of lady blue balls. "Can't the others take care of it?"

"I gotta deal with this," Ryder said.

"Wait, is that Isla? I thought you two broke up?" Jake asked.

"We did," I said.

"Can I get a turn next?" Jake asks.

Before I could even respond, Ryder had his hand around Jake's throat and tossed him from the closet. Jake slammed into the wall in the hallway, then slid to the ground.

"Don't you dare disrespect what is mine," Ryder said with a growl.

"Dude, I'm sorry," Jake said as he slowly stood up. He lifted his hands in front of him. "I didn't mean anything by it."

"Get out of here," Ryder snapped. "I'll deal with you later."

I tugged on my restraints, trying to free myself. "What the fuck was that bullshit? This was a hookup, nothing more."

Ryder's upper lip twitched, and I could see the dangerous golden glow in his eyes. I wasn't just talking to Ryder; I was also getting a taste of his wolf. *Fuck.* That was the last thing I needed. If he shifted in here, he'd probably rip me to shreds. I'd only seen his wolf once during an accidental shift, and if his father hadn't interfered, I'd be dead. He'd spent the next several weeks sending me gifts and apologizing. But we weren't a couple now and his dad wasn't around to help me.

"Ryder, unbind me now," I said, changing tactics. I could deal with his possessive behavior later.

He scoffed. "I'm not done with you."

"Oh, yes you are. Untie me right now," I snapped, risking his wolf.

He closed the distance between us, and his hand closed around my throat. I gasped for air and my eyes widened in surprise. Ryder had never hurt me. Where was this coming from? Panic gripped me and I swayed and turned, trying to break his hold.

"You are mine, you understand me?" He released his grip. I sucked in air, not taking my eyes off his. That feral glow was still there, still simmering under the surface. This was his wolf speaking, not him. When he cooled down, he'd be back to normal. There was no dealing with him now.

"Untie me," I said as gently as I could.

He smirked. "I don't think so. I'll be back to finish this later."

"Not funny, Ryder. Untie me now!" I screamed after him, no longer caring who heard me. Everyone would know by the end of the night anyway, since Jake had seen us together. Ryder pulled his clothes on, ignoring my cries.

"Ryder! Untie me, you asshole!" I yelled at his retreating form.

The door closed, and I screamed in frustration until my throat hurt.

Nobody opened the door.

Fuck me. How did I let myself get into this situation?

Lesson learned, never hook up with an ex. I was going to kill him when he came back.

# CHAPTER
# SIX

Isla

Music still pounded in the distance and I knew that eventually, Sarah was going to open this door to retrieve someone's coat. She was vapid, but she'd probably be willing to untie me. She might even offer to take my place. My stomach rolled at the thought.

When the door finally opened, I hissed against the light. Squinting, I tried to make out who had opened the door. "Sarah?"

The figure came into clearer view and I could tell it was a male, but it didn't look like Ryder. This male wore a gold mask and carried himself differently. Just my fucking luck. "Whoever you are, I'm not here for your entertainment. You can either untie me and move on, or you can get the fuck out."

I was greeted with a deep, sexy laugh. "Well, well, what do we have here?"

I didn't recognize the voice. "You can either untie me or get the fuck out."

"I got that the first time you said it," he replied.

My eyes had adjusted enough now that I could make out his features. He was wearing a crisp white button up shirt that looked perfectly tailored to his broad chest and strong shoulders. His black slacks looked equally well made and expensive. The outfit was a complete contrast to the rest of his appearance. Dark, wild hair, dark stubble over a strong jaw, and earrings in both ears. A few tattoos were visible under his collar, but they were mostly covered, so I couldn't make them out.

I caught his eyes and sucked in a breath. Through the golden half mask he wore, I could clearly make out his eyes. They pulled me like a pool of liquid silver, urging me to fall into those depths until I drowned. He was a predator, something dangerous and savage.

Maybe I wanted dangerous.

Something about him made my breath catch and sent a surge of desire through me. Maybe it was the fact that I was naked and left wanting, or maybe it was because he was the most handsome male I'd ever seen. Logic didn't work. My mind felt sluggish and foggy. I couldn't form any other thoughts except the desire to have him pick up exactly where Ryder had left off. If not for my bound arms, I might have melted into a puddle on the ground.

He approached slowly, a smirk on his lips that made me wonder if he knew exactly what I was thinking. He had to be supernatural, probably a shifter from another pack. There was no doubt he could smell my arousal, the aftermath of of how ready I was for Ryder. It was times like this that I was reminded of just how weak I was compared to them. I was fragile and easily broken. They were beasts who could snap my neck without effort.

The man in the gold mask inched forward and my heart raced, my traitorous body sending my hormones into overdrive. I wanted to feel that stubble against my skin; I wanted to taste his mouth and run my hands over his body.

Fighting against my inner slut, I tried to steady myself, but it made my breath come out in pants. What the fuck was wrong with me? "Leave me alone."

He smirked. "Is that really what you want?"

"Untie me," I said, but there wasn't much bite in my command. My words were breathless and shallow.

I considered calling for Sarah, but if he was in here, she probably hadn't returned. Also, there was a part of me that didn't want her to intervene. I was curious about what he'd do when he reached me.

The stranger walked with feline grace, each step emitting power and strength. It wasn't the same as the wolves I spent most of my time with. I narrowed my eyes. "Are you a tiger shifter?" I should be worried about the fact that I was tied up and naked. I should feel ashamed that I was on full display for someone I didn't know. Instead, I wanted to know more about him.

I was broken.

Something must have snapped when Ryder tied me up. This wasn't like me, but I wasn't sure I wanted to turn this side of me off.

One corner of his lips curved in a rather vicious smirk. "I'm something more dangerous, Love."

I sucked in a breath at the term of endearment. There was an edge of an accent and the word came out sexy and familiar. Even though he probably used the term on every female he met, it felt like he'd used it just for me. I hated that he was able to practically undo me with a single word. He was more dangerous than I realized. He was different. And I needed to get away. "Untie me."

He approached slowly, stopping when he was nearly touching me. My whole body seemed to heat in response to his proximity. I fought the rising flush, hoping he couldn't tell exactly how hard I was fighting my desire for him. None of it made sense. It had to be lingering feelings from Ryder.

His fingers were cold against my skin and he leaned closer as he worked the belt free. I sucked in a breath, inhaling his scent. He smelled clean and warm. Like cedar and honey. But under that warmth was a touch of musk that was primal and dark. It made me squirm a little. *Fuck.* What was it with this male?

My arms fell to my sides, finally free of their bindings. I

rubbed each wrist absentmindedly while I stared at the stranger. "Thank you."

His eyes swept up and down my body, but his gaze didn't feel driven by lust. I could have sworn he was checking to see if I had any injuries. I shook the thought from my head. Of course, that wasn't the case. He was a male, and I was a naked woman. He was checking me out, nothing more. Still, I was oddly self-assured under his stare.

"Do you need me to call someone for you?" he offered.

"No, I'm fine," I said.

He grunted. "If someone else had found you..."

I didn't want to consider it. Even Jake had asked for a turn. What if Ryder had left me here and let his friends take over? I shuddered.

That's when I noticed that the stranger was holding my discarded dress in his hand, offering it to me.

I stepped closer to him, reaching for the bundle of wrinkled fabric. Our hands brushed, and I gasped as a jolt surged through me. Swallowing hard, I wrote it off as nothing more than static electricity.

"Your boyfriend is a dick," he said.

"He's not my boyfriend," I said.

"Does he know that?"

I grabbed the dress. "He does."

"His scent is all over you," he said.

I blinked a few times and recalled the way Ryder had treated me. He'd tied me up and made sure I was enjoying his touch. He'd threatened his friend. My eyes widened. He thought this meant we were together. *Shit*. This had been a ploy to get me back. That was the angle. I should have seen it coming.

"If you want to get rid of it, you should find someone else to bed. It'll cover his scent," he said.

"Like you?" I crossed my arms over my chest. So that was his play.

He smirked. "You don't want me. I'm not a good guy."

"Liar," I said.

"You don't know me. If you did, you'd run," he said.

I tugged my dress over my head and ran my fingers through my hair, trying to make it look like I hadn't been off getting laid. Disappointment tugged in my gut. I'd wanted it tonight, but the night hadn't turned out the way I expected.

"Do you need a ride or anything?" he asked.

"I'm not going to let that prick ruin my night," I said.

He grinned. "Good."

I fought like hell to keep my eyes off him as I walked out of the coat closet, back to the party.

Ryder wasn't in sight. Neither was the alpha or any of the higher-ranking wolves. The dance floor was filled with lower-ranking younger males and females, both human and shifter, who didn't have any actual involvement in the pack. Whatever had taken Ryder away was big. I knew I'd be dealing with it at work on Monday, but I wasn't at work now.

Determined to get him out of my head and salvage the night, I accepted dances from several males I hardly knew. Most of them so low ranking that our paths never crossed. I had no power within the official pack, but since I worked directly for the alpha, I was more familiar with his inner circle. Plus, there was that whole dating the future alpha thing.

Denny was about my age, an up and comer, who followed Ryder around, hoping for a chance to break in. He was funny and polite and I was just starting to enjoy the time with him when his hand went from my hip to the slit on my dress, then around to my bare ass.

I shoved him. "What the fuck, Denny?"

"Oh, come on, Isla. Look at you, look at that dress. Don't tell me you don't want me," he said.

I lifted a brow, and anger surged. "My dress is not an invitation for you to touch me without my permission."

"You know you liked it," he said.

I stepped away. "Fuck you."

He charged forward, forcing his mouth onto mine, pinning my arms to my side with that shifter strength. I squirmed and screamed into his mouth before shoving him off me. With a step toward him, I punched him in the face.

"Fuck," I hissed, shaking out my sore hand. It had been years since I punched anyone. I'd forgotten how bad it hurt.

"You bitch!" Denny swung for me and before I could

dodge, he was yanked backward. Then he was flying across the room until he landed hard on the ground.

Denny scrambled to his feet and charged forward. Right for the male who had released me earlier. The stranger moved fast, getting Denny into a choke hold before he could throw a punch.

"Apologize to the lady," the stranger said with a growl. He turned so Denny was facing me.

Face red, struggling for air, Denny's eyes bulged as he stared at me.

"I said *apologize*," the stranger repeated.

Denny's hands clawed at the stranger's arms, desperate for breath.

"It's fine," I said. "Just let him go."

"It's not fine. You said no and this asshole continued." He looked at Denny. "Did you hear me? She said *no*."

"I'm. Sorry." Denny's words were strained, and he sputtered for breath. "I'm. Sorry."

"That's better," the stranger said. "You so much as look at her in a way that offends her, I'll snap your neck. Do you understand me?"

"Yes," Denny hissed. His arms fell limp by his side and his face was purple.

The stranger released him, throwing him to the side like he was a piece of trash. I wish I could say I felt bad for Denny, but there was a part of me that enjoyed watching him squirm. I know that made me no better than the monsters I lived with, but I didn't care right now.

The shifters were more powerful than us humans.

There were too many stories of humans who were forced into situations they didn't want. Nobody ever stood up for us.

Denny scrambled to his feet, and the crowd divided to create a gap between us. He doubled over, panting as he caught his breath. When he stood, he looked at me with a terrified expression before averting his eyes.

"Get out of here," the stranger said.

A few of Denny's friends gathered around him and walked him away. I wasn't sad to see him go.

"Prick," I hissed.

The music started again, and everyone went back to what they'd been doing before. It wasn't the first time someone had been thrown across the room in the middle of a party. Nobody was even looking at me anymore. Nobody except the stranger.

My heart pounded against my ribs so loudly I was sure he could hear it over the din. "I swear I'm not usually a damsel in distress."

He chuckled softly. "I believe you. I have no doubt you could have kicked his ass if I let you be."

"I'm not sure about that. Humans are always at a disadvantage," I admitted. "But I would have given him hell."

His brow furrowed. "What is a human doing around all these shifters?"

I cocked my head to the side. Surely he knew how it worked. All the packs were like this. Humans were few in Lost Harbor, but they weren't free. We belonged to a pack, or the vampires, or the witches. None of the humans were stupid enough to sell themselves to the fae. A few humans, like my mom, paid protection but were still allied with a specific pack. None of us could avoid choosing a side.

Many of the humans had a history of magic in their families long ago. Shifters who stopped shifting, or witches who couldn't call their magic. That was my family's lot. Several generations ago, we'd been like them. But someone had mingled with human blood and over the centuries, it was watered down to the point where none of that power survived. I wasn't even sure what kind of creature had been in our past. My mom didn't like to talk about it.

"I suppose you can thank my mom for that. She aligned with the wolves, so that's who she chose to sell me to." I shrugged, pretending it didn't bother me.

"Sold?"

"You're not from around here, are you?" It was the only explanation.

"I'm just visiting on business," he said.

We didn't get a lot of visitors. Creatures with magical abilities could get through the wards. It was us humans who were trapped. It was why leaving was such a big deal. It could only be done once a year, when the veil was thinnest on the first new moon after the summer solstice. It was when I was going to finally get out of here.

He extended his hand. "Would you like to dance?"

I hesitated as alarm bells rang in my mind. My body didn't want to resist. It already wanted all of him. After what I'd just been through with Ryder and Denny, I should flee. I was not making wise decisions about males tonight. But something wouldn't let me. I wanted to stay with him.

"Didn't you warn me about you?" I asked.

He shrugged. "I'm the last person you should take advice from."

It was another warning, another chance for me to walk away. Instead, I accepted his offered hand and let him pull me in close to move to the slower pace of the music.

His hands were strong and confident as he held me, his steps effortless, even when I stepped on his toes.

"You're just as graceful as the last human I danced with," he said.

"Do you dance with humans often?" I asked.

"There weren't a lot of supernaturals around where I was," he said.

My heart raced at that bit of information. "Where were you? Living with humans or another warded city?" My tone was too eager.

He chuckled. "So many questions, Love."

A shiver ran down my spine. There was that word again. It shouldn't do anything for me, but gods help me, it did. "My name is Isla."

"I know," he whispered.

My brow furrowed. "I don't know your name."

"I have been called many things," he said.

"Is *cocky asshole* one of them?" I asked.

"In fact, it is," he grinned.

I should be completely turned off by his behavior, but

it only made me want him more. Something was very wrong with me. But maybe he was perfect. He was a stranger, likely passing through. Nobody knew him, which meant nobody would talk. There was an excellent chance I'd never see him again. And with our masks, it made it even harder to distinguish who he really was.

"You look like you want to take a bite out of me," he teased.

"Maybe I do," I said.

"You'll regret it, but if you ask, I'm not going to turn you down," he said. "I'm dangerous."

"That's the third time you've warned me to stay away," I pointed out.

"And yet, you're still dancing with me."

"Maybe I want to live dangerously." I stopped dancing and led him away from the party, not caring how many eyes were on us as we left.

I wasn't sure if I was trying to undo the terrible situation with Ryder, or if it was the strange pull I felt toward this male. Whatever it was, it felt bigger than me. As if I didn't have a choice. I just wanted him.

All the upstairs bedrooms were occupied. I almost took it as a sign to regain my senses and not engage in a one-night-stand with someone I didn't know, but my companion opened a door revealing a coat closet.

My insides tensed. I'd been in the coat check room with Ryder and the hall coat closet wasn't much different. He closed the door. "Maybe it's best if I take you home."

He'd seen the terror in my expression and he was

going to let me go. It was the opposite of how Ryder had treated me. He was giving me a choice, despite his warnings. I wasn't sure he was the bad guy he thought he was.

I shook my head, then opened the door and stepped inside, pulling him in after me.

# CHAPTER
## SEVEN

Isla

THE CLOSET WAS full of fur coats and smelled like wool and perfume. It was much smaller than the coat room, but the cozy furs hanging in the back were soft and luxurious, making the space feel almost welcoming. When the door closed behind him, I didn't panic as I worried I might. It was completely dark, but I felt oddly safe in here with him. It was stupid, and I might regret it, but this was my choice. And he wasn't Ryder.

I set my hand on his chest, feeling the hard muscles under the crisp shirt and my other hand moved lower, resting on his hip. I slid my fingers up his chest, to his jaw, my thumb brushing against the rough stubble before sliding to the back of his head. It didn't take much urging to get him to lower his face to mine.

Our lips met in a tenuous, tender kiss. It was sweet and cautious, the opposite of what I expected. As soon as his hands gripped my sides, I forgot about Ryder. I forgot about anything outside of the dark space. My lips parted and our tongues met. He deepened the kiss as his fingers began to work their way down. I could feel him gathering the fabric of my dress. My pulse raced and wetness pooled as I anticipated release.

I needed this.

I needed to feel alive this way. I couldn't trust anyone in the pack not to kiss and tell, but this male wasn't pack. Even if everyone knew we hooked up, he wouldn't be meeting up with the wolves and spilling the intimate details. And what did I care if he told some tiger shifters or whatever he was. We only mixed with the other packs once a year, and by next year, I'd be long gone.

Quickly, I worked the buttons on his shirt, needing him to be just as naked as I was about to be. I couldn't be the only one fully undressed again. A little flicker of panic surged, and I hesitated, wondering if I should do this. He stepped back, releasing my dress as if he knew I was questioning my choice.

I heard clothing landing in a pile on the floor. Holding my breath, I inched forward and felt into the dark. I was met with bare skin, smooth and hard. His hand flattened on top of mine and guided me lower, as if showing me just how bare he was. Over taught abs, down to the silky softness of his protruding length. I closed my hand around it and he groaned, releasing his hand from mine.

My dress still covered me, yet he was completely exposed. Making him the vulnerable one. A thrill roared, and I bit down on my lip, savoring the sense of power. I moved my hand, sliding it up and down along his length. He hissed out a breath. "Wicked girl."

For some reason, his words sounded like encouragement, egging me on to do more. Licking my lips, I continued the motions, feeling the beads of wetness forming at the tip. He groaned, then leaned forward, his large hand tangling into my hair, moving my face closer to him. His mouth captured mine in a deep, intense kiss that I felt to my very core. My hand stilled, too distracted by his mouth to continue.

When his hand moved to my thigh, I arched into him. He understood what I was asking, and suddenly I was in his arms, his hands gripping my ass. The softness was gone from our kiss, replaced by something dark and unyielding. I moaned into his mouth, tightening my legs around his waist.

He shoved the fabric of my dress up so I was bare against him, my pussy already slick and ready. When he entered me, I moaned, tossing my head back as the fullness stretched me in the best way. It was so primal, so instinctual. My back arched, and he held me with his strong hands as he continued to thrust into me. Fur coats enveloped us as we reached the wall. It was like having cushions behind me, supporting me as he continued to pound into me, each thrust moving me closer to the edge.

He growled, then buried his face into my neck, kissing,

sucking, licking the sensitive skin. When his teeth brushed against my shoulder, I exploded, my body shaking as wave after wave of orgasm claimed me. A moment later and he grunted as he had his own release.

His face was buried against my neck, his arms pulled me into an intimate embrace. My legs were hooked around his waist and his length still filled me. Wrapped together, we caught our breath, taking our time to recover.

It had been a frenzy, an overwhelming urge to be with him. Now that it was over, I didn't want to let go.

This whole being single thing was getting to me. I hadn't realized how lonely I was. How much I'd needed that physical closeness of another person.

His hips moved as he slid out of me and felt his grip loosen. Gently, he guided my legs back to the ground. I couldn't see a thing in the darkness, but I could feel his gaze. As if he was staring into my very soul. "Who are you?" I whispered.

He answered my question with a brush of his lips against mine. "I'm no good for you, Isla."

"I can make those decisions for myself," I said.

He paused, as if waiting for me to say more. Knots twisted in my gut when I realized I couldn't give him more. I was leaving here in a matter of months. I wasn't girlfriend material.

The sound of rustling fabric was too loud in the tiny room. I knew he was leaving, and somehow, I knew if I said the words, I could stop him.

But that wasn't my plan. This was fun. It didn't mean anything. It couldn't.

The door opened. "I'll go first. If you wait a few minutes, you can probably return without anyone knowing."

My heart felt like it shattered just a little as he closed the door behind him.

I blinked, then shook my head. What the fuck was wrong with me? He hadn't been *that* good. Blowing out a breath, I steadied myself. Then I smoothed out my dress and hair before slipping out the door into the empty hallway.

My knees still felt a little weak as I entered my apartment. Maddie was on the couch and managed to turn her attention away from the sappy romance on the TV to stare at me as I strode into the room. She looked around, as if checking to see if I brought anyone with me. "Back so soon?"

"Things didn't go exactly as planned." I didn't really want to explain the hookup with a stranger. Since he was from some other pack, there could be a sense of mystery around what happened when the two of us left. Most of the partygoers would probably be too drunk to remember much by morning.

A little shiver trailed down my spine at the memory of that brief encounter. It was good that I would never see him again, because I wanted to. It didn't make sense. I didn't even know him, but I was interested. He was a distraction that I didn't need.

"I thought for sure that dress was a guarantee." Maddie held up the bag of Cheetos. "Hungry?"

"I'm surprised you didn't finish the bag." I sat down next to her and grabbed the snacks. I was hungry.

Maddie sniffed, then leaned closer to me, sniffing again.

I leaned away from her. "What are you doing?"

"There's a strange smell. Someone besides you." She lifted her eyebrows in silent accusation. "It doesn't smell like Ryder."

"I'm not sure if I'm more disturbed by the fact that you know what my boyfriend smells like or the fact that you're smelling me at all," I said.

"Boyfriend?" Her eyes widened.

"Ex. Still ex," I said, too quickly. "And if you must know, things started, but we were interrupted when they had to go and do some kind of official pack business."

"I thought there was no business tonight?" Maddie shook her head. "Must have been something big."

I popped a Cheeto into my mouth. "I'm sure I'll get all of the details at work on Monday."

Maddie sniffed again. "It really is a strange smell. It doesn't even smell like a wolf."

I tensed. She was scenting the other male, whatever he had been. "You do recall that all types of shifters are welcome at the party?"

"It doesn't smell shifter." She shook her head. "But

what do I know? My senses aren't as strong as some shifters. I could be way off."

I handed back the bag of chips and rose from the couch. "On that note, I'm going to take a shower and go to bed. Don't stay up too late moping."

"Night." Maddie resumed her show, and I retreated to the privacy of my bedroom, my skin still tingling.

# CHAPTER
# EIGHT

Isla

IT WAS noon by the time someone knocked on the door to my office. I reluctantly looked away from my work. "Yeah?"

The door opened and Ryder walked in. I glared at him. "I'm not in the mood, Ryder."

"That's not what you said Friday night." He strolled into the room and took a seat in the chair facing my desk.

"You left me in the coat check room tied up," I reminded him.

"Foreplay," he said casually.

"Not at all. Anyone could have found me," I snapped.

"Someone did find you, didn't they?" He leaned forward, a curious brow lifted.

"Fortunately for me, someone untied me and let me

go. I hate to think what might have happened if one of your thug friends found me." I shook my head.

Ryder's voice lowered. "None of them will touch you. They know you belong to me."

I scoffed. "I don't belong to you. We broke up. What the fuck is wrong with you, Ryder?" Our break up had been uneventful. We'd been on good terms since then. It wasn't like we hung out, but we saw each other often and were polite. There had never been a sign of jealously or interest in getting me back. Not that I'd take him back.

"You haven't been with anyone since me," he pointed out. "That has to mean something."

I swallowed, hoping he couldn't scent the unsaid bit about how I'd hooked up with the stranger who'd freed me. Or the fact that I'd dreamed about fucking him. It wasn't any of Ryder's business who I was with, but I knew better than to throw that in his face.

"Maybe it just means I'm not happy with just sticking my dick in any wet hole I can find," I said.

He growled. "I don't stick my dick in any wet hole."

I smirked. "Unlike you, I haven't been tracking your sex life, but unfortunately the ladies you hook up with keep finding me to tell me."

"So you know I'm desirable. I'm the next alpha, Isla. You're not even a shifter. You have no idea the kind of protection I could offer you. An alpha has never taken a human as his partner before," he said.

"I told you, I can't marry you. I can't give you what you want," I said.

"I thought if I gave you some time, you'd see things clearly and forgive me for my mistake," he said.

I laughed. "Wait, the last six months was supposed to be you giving me time to forgive you?"

"What else would it be?" he asked. "I told you I wanted you."

"You don't want me; you want someone compliant and obedient. Choose any of the other girls you've been with in the time you were supposedly waiting for me to forgive you," I said.

"So that's what this is about? You know shifters have a high sex drive. It wasn't personal. It was just sex," he said.

"Ryder. Get it through your head. I'm never getting back together with you," I snapped.

He went rigid and his jaw tightened. His eyes flashed gold, a sign the beast that lurked within him was stirring. I swear the air in the room felt like it was suddenly charged with sizzling electricity. Tension swirled around us and I waited for his next move. I might talk big, but I was no match for a wolf shifter in either form. I'd fight like hell if I had to, but in the end, I was just human.

Slowly, Ryder stood. "Is that your final decision? I will not offer this again."

"It hasn't changed," I said, my voice more gentle this time, so I didn't piss off his wolf. "It's been over."

He nodded. "Very well. You are no longer under my protection."

My brow furrowed. "What are you talking about?"

"You heard me," he said. "Everyone in the pack knew

that you were mine. They knew the consequences if they harmed you."

"I work for the alpha." Over the years, I'd earned my place here. Nobody had harmed me in a long while. Even before Ryder and I had started dating. I was off limits for another reason that had nothing to do with his male ego. I was damn good at my job and the alpha knew it. "I think I'll be okay."

"I hope so." He turned and left my office, closing the door behind him.

After a long moment to make sure he'd really left, I blew out a breath. I'd dodged a serious bullet by not agreeing to marry him. Ryder had never showed any signs of being the typical alpha hole. But his wolf was maturing, and he was stepping into his power more. He was letting it get to his head, as so many others had.

Part of me felt bad for not accepting his offer, but I didn't love him. I wasn't sure I ever truly had. Plus, what kind of life would it be for me? A human married to the alpha? I'd be left out of half the events and unable to ever run with him in wolf form. It was a doomed relationship from the beginning.

The door to my office opened, and I jumped from my chair, expecting to see Ryder. Instead, it was Henry, his father, and the Crescent Pack's alpha.

"Hey, boss," I said with a false cheer in my tone.

He grunted, then scanned the room as if looking for someone.

"Ryder just left," I said.

"You turned him down?" Henry asked.

I nodded. "Sorry."

"Don't be. I told him to break up with you back when you two started getting serious. He shouldn't be with a human. At least you have the sense to see that," he said.

His comment was insulting, but I didn't have a death wish. I might snap back at Ryder, but I'd seen Henry rip someone's head from their body. I didn't talk back to him. Ever.

"I need you to pick up the payments from Marcus. He's two months late," he said.

"Isn't that a job for one of your goons?" I asked.

"Marcus's shop and house are warded and he won't come out. I need someone he won't recognize," Henry said.

"You need someone without a supernatural signature," I deadpanned.

"That too," he said. "None of the shifters can get in."

"You want me, a lowly human, to shake down a wolf shifter who is behind on his payments?" I put my hand on my hip. "Are you trying to get me killed?"

"Take Jimmy with you. If Marcus attacks, lead him through the wards and Jimmy will get the payment for you."

I didn't need to ask for clarification on the type of payment Jimmy would take. He was Henry's most brutal enforcer. I'd seen him do things that gave me nightmares. And I never once had a nightmare about watching an entire head ripped from someone's shoulders. The things Jimmy could do left a stain on your very soul.

"This isn't an option; it's an order," Henry said, clearly sensing my hesitation. "You're no longer important to Ryder. Which means you're just another human."

"Are you fucking kidding me?" So much for not talking back. "I've been fixing your books for you for eight years. Since I took over, you haven't been called to the Supernatural Council once. I am extremely valuable."

"You think you're the only one who can make my books look legit? You're here because my son was fucking you," he said.

"Not the whole time," I pointed out. "You kept me because my work speaks for itself."

He stalked forward and slapped me across the face. I gasped, so surprised that I didn't even reach up to put a hand over my stinging cheek. "What the fuck?" Eyes watering, I stared him down, not wanting to show how much fear was now coursing through my veins. I hadn't been hit in years. And Henry had never touched me.

"You got soft. You forgot the order of things. You work for me. I own you." Henry lifted his hand. "Do I need to hit you again or did that first one jog your memory?"

"I got it," I said.

"Good. Now go get me my money," he said.

Jaw clenched and hands curled into fists, I stormed from the room. Henry was right. I'd forgotten just how brutal things around here could be for humans. I'd had a reprieve for a few years when I took over the books because the previous accountant had been so bad, the pack had been in trouble with the Council every year. Then Ryder and I had started dating. It had been at least five years since anyone set hands on me.

It was almost the solstice. I just had to endure and survive for a few months, then I would be free of all of them. If anything, I should be grateful for the reminder of why I had to leave. I didn't belong here. I wasn't one of these monsters.

Jimmy was in the garage. Covered in grease, sweat beaded on his forehead, focused on the Harley he was fixing. With his long hair and full beard, he looked like a freaking Viking. If I didn't know how dangerous he was, I might be interested in him as a revenge fuck. At six feet, he was one of the shorter members of the pack, but he made up for it in solid muscle. He never missed a day at the gym, that was for damn sure.

He looked up, locking his blue eyes on me. His long blonde hair was pulled back into a tail at the nape of his neck. "What do you want?"

"Henry sent me," I said. "You're supposed to go with me to get the money from Marcus."

He rose, all six glorious feet of him. His long sleeve tee was rolled up high on his forearms and I could see tattoos covering every inch of his bare skin. "He's got wards on his place."

"That's why Henry's sending me," I said.

Jimmy laughed. "So you turned the future alpha down once and for all."

"How the fuck does everyone know about that?" I asked.

"We all knew he was giving you some time. But time's up, sweetheart." Jimmy wiped his hands on a towel, then tossed it to the floor. "Let me know when you're ready to follow in your mama's footsteps and I'll be happy to help you get started."

"It's never going to happen," I said.

"That's the same thing your mama said," he sneered. "They all say that. But human women have two choices in this pack. They either marry a shifter, or they work on their backs. And nobody is going to wife the alpha's ex."

"I didn't come to hear you ramble about things nobody cares about," I snapped. "We have a job to do."

"Good point. There is a third option. Marcus might tear your throat out and you'll be dead before you get too desperate," he said.

I rolled my eyes. "Are you done?"

He tossed me a helmet. "Let's go."

# CHAPTER
# NINE

Isla

JIMMY TOOK every corner fast and hard, my leg nearly brushing the asphalt. The Crescent Pack loved their bikes, so I'd grown up around them. Usually, they were more cautious and slower when driving with a mortal on board, but not Jimmy. It was as if he wanted to let me know he wasn't going to do anything to keep me safe if this went south.

Message heard, loud and clear. I was officially on my own. If Marcus decided to take his anger out on me, I wasn't going to get any help from Jimmy. Henry had to have known. If I lured Marcus out, Jimmy would likely make an example of him as a way of showing Henry's authority, but not because I was in danger.

These damn shifters sure lived for the fucking drama.

I resisted the urge to squeeze my thighs tighter around Jimmy's hips as he took another sharp turn. I kept my arms around his waist loose and light, not wanting him to get the satisfaction of knowing that pure terror gripped me with each reckless turn. Holding my breath, I released it as soon as we straightened. The bike was nearly horizontal on each turn. And Jimmy took the route with the most turns possible. Asshole.

When we finally arrived at Marcus's crumbling house, I was more than ready to scramble off the bike. It took more self-control than I'd admit to act causally. After I removed the helmet, I set it on the back of the bike, then ran my fingers through my long brown hair. Out of the corner of my eye, I caught Jimmy watching me as if waiting for me to scold him. I wasn't going to play into his game.

"I haven't been here in a while," I commented.

"I avoid it if I can," Jimmy said.

My feet crunched on the gravel that served as a driveway. Rusty cars on cinderblocks were surrounded by tall, yellow grass that nearly reclaimed the vehicles. They'd been there as long as I could remember, never moving. Occasionally a new car took up residence, but the overall abandoned nature made it feel more like a graveyard than garage.

Marcus was the only mechanic who worked on cars in the pack. Most of the shifters around here used motorcycles for primary transportation, but the reverence they had for the machines meant nobody but the owner fixed them up.

Still, cars had their uses, and Marcus was necessary. I knew he dabbled in other, less legitimate businesses and paid Henry protection to keep that business hidden. Even with my access to all the financial documents of the pack, I wasn't sure what he had his hands in. A shiver ran down my spine. I wasn't sure I wanted to know. Based on the monthly fee, it was lucrative and very, very illegal.

To my right was a four-bay garage, all the doors closed. On my left was the dilapidated home where Marcus lived. By the looks of the place, you'd never guess he was running something big. I think that was part of his cover. I wasn't sure where he funneled the rest of his money, but it wasn't going to cover the house.

Peeling paint and shredded screens made the home look just as abandoned as the cars. I glanced around, half expecting to see Marcus walk out, covered in grease to greet us.

"What are you waiting for? Go in there and demand that payment," Jimmy said.

"What makes you think he's even in there? Maybe he finally took all that money he makes with his side hustle and fled," I said with a shrug.

Jimmy grunted. "Well, I guess that's what you're here to figure out."

I huffed, annoyed that I had to be here instead of doing my work. As I walked to the front door, I pushed away the rising anxiety. Marcus was probably gone. He hadn't paid in two months, and he knew the consequences. He'd be an idiot to skip payment to Henry.

I heard the crunch of gravel and knew that Jimmy was walking around the property. For all I knew, he'd get on his bike and leave me here. That thought eliminated my hesitation. I just wanted to get this over with and get out of here. Quickly, I turned the handle, surprised to find the front door unlocked.

The scent of the house filled my nostrils, and I gagged, having to swallow back the urge to vomit. Flies swarmed around old food left out on the coffee table and there was trash and debris everywhere. I didn't need to walk around the rest of the house to know that he was either no longer physically here, or his body was rotting somewhere in the house.

Stepping back into the fresh air, I turned to Jimmy. "You might want to see this."

Jimmy sauntered over, his nose twitching as he neared the open front door. If I was ready to puke from the stench, it had to be a million times worse with shifter senses. I had to bite down on the inside of my cheek to keep from smiling at that thought. Jimmy deserved the full dose after what he'd put me through on the ride over.

He stepped into the entryway, then glanced back at me. "You think we'll find the body?"

"Probably. Would explain why he hasn't paid Henry," I said.

Jimmy strode into the house, and I took that as my cue to leave. If it wasn't warded against supernaturals, there was no reason for me to be here. Jimmy could handle a peek around the house and I'd wait for the ride back to the office.

Outside, I looked around at the huge property Marcus had owned. He'd treated it like shit, but it was a massive amount of land in a prime location. I knew I'd be filing paperwork and forging documents to make sure the property passed to the Crescent Pack's holdings upon his death if Henry hadn't already had Marcus will this to the pack in the past.

My eyes lingered on the closed garage doors, and my brow furrowed. It was so odd to see them closed. Even in bad weather, he'd left them open. I wasn't sure I'd ever seen them closed.

"House is empty, but I found his cash stash, so Henry still gets paid," Jimmy announced. "He might have fled town, like you guessed. Or maybe one of his clients finally took him out."

"No way he'd take off and leave a wad of cash sitting out where anyone could find it." I pointed to the garage. "You ever seen those doors closed?"

"No." Jimmy walked past me toward the garage, and I followed.

"When was the last time anyone saw Marcus?" I asked.

"Not sure. I don't associate with shifters in his line of work," he said.

My brow furrowed at that bit of information, and I tucked it away for later. Whatever Marcus did outside the law, it crossed a line for Jimmy. And Jimmy was into some pretty sketchy shit.

"We should go," Jimmy said.

"Shouldn't we check the garage? What if he's in there?" My stomach twisted. "Henry told us to find him."

"He just wanted his money," Jimmy said.

"He will expect to get paid again next month and I don't want to come back here." I walked to the garage and started pulling on one of the handles. It squeaked a little but hardly moved for me. It was a lot harder to lift than I thought.

"You're not going to drop this, are you?" Jimmy asked.

"I don't like leaving my office to go investigate why someone hasn't paid," I said. "As much of a joy as you are to be around, I'd rather not repeat this trip with you."

He grunted, then pushed me aside. I stepped back, annoyed but grateful he was going to check before we went. Jimmy hauled the metal doors open with ease. It groaned and clanked as if it hadn't been used in a long while. I followed Jimmy into the garage, noting the fact that there were two nice looking cars sitting in the first two bays.

"Mother fucker," Jimmy said.

I caught sight of it just then. The body hanging from the ceiling. It was emaciated, like looking at a mummy without the bandages. Translucent skin stretched across bones, making the body more skeleton than person. Under the body was a dark puddle, long since dried up, but it didn't matter that it wasn't fresh. Whoever this was, they'd been left to bleed out. Their blood must have poured from their body for days. Maybe weeks. Until there was nothing left.

I heard the sound of Jimmy retching, and my own stomach rolled with nausea. Instead of waiting to empty everything, I bolted from the garage. The fresh air and sunlight helped ease some of the queasy sensation, but I was panting and sweating. I leaned over, resting my elbows on my knees, letting myself suck in deep breaths.

Footsteps made me jump, and I turned to see Jimmy walking back out, wiping a hand across his mouth. "We've got a big problem."

"Who would do that to him?" I asked. "What exactly was he involved in?"

"That wasn't Marcus," Jimmy said. "That was a vampire. And it's not the first body we've found."

"What are you talking about?" I asked. "Vampires don't bother with our territory. Why would one wander in here and who would be stupid enough to bleed one dry?"

"I don't know. But we have to get rid of this body before the vamps find out or we're all fucked." Jimmy pulled his cell phone out of his pocket and made a call.

# CHAPTER
# TEN

*Isla*

Henry, Ryder, and Derek arrived in an unassuming car that looked like something one of the humans would drive. I wasn't sure I'd seen Henry ever drive a car. It seemed that they didn't want anyone to know they were here.

The three shifters left the vehicle and quietly walked toward where Jimmy and I were waiting near the garage. I'd positioned myself to the side so the emaciated body wasn't in my line of sight.

"Did you touch anything?" Henry asked.

"Waited for you, boss," Jimmy said. "It looks the same as the one from the other night."

"Is that why you ran off?" I asked, directing my question at Ryder.

He nodded.

"Two dead vampires?" I asked. "Was the other one bled out like this?"

"Yeah, but you keep this to yourself," Henry said, his tone threatening.

"I got it," I snapped. "But who would be stupid enough to do this?"

"Those vamps aren't allowed on our territory. We have the right to defend ourselves," Derek said.

"That's not self-defense. That's fucked up serial killer shit," I said.

"How was he bound?" Ryder asked.

"Silver chains," Jimmy said.

"Any signs of wolf shifter blood on the bindings?" Henry asked.

"I didn't look that close," Jimmy admitted.

Henry nodded, and they all understood the silent command. I stayed where I was while the four shifters headed back into the garage. This was way above my pay grade.

Muffled conversation piqued my interest, and I inched forward, mentally preparing myself to see the body. The shifters were lowering it down, then they set it on the ground.

"See the scarring on the wrists? And the remains of blood on the chains," Henry pointed out.

"You think it was Marcus?" Ryder asked. "He didn't seem the type, but why else would he leave?"

"The real question is, was the other one also Marcus or are we looking for someone else?" Derek asked.

"You're telling me he was storing his blood to use it on vampires?" Jimmy sounded skeptical.

"That's a good point," Ryder said. "He couldn't have gotten this much blood at once. If it was his, he'd have it stashed somewhere."

"That's disgusting," Derek said.

Jimmy's shoulders tensed, and I wondered if he was going to vomit again. Who knew he had such a weak stomach?

"Go check the house," Henry commanded. "See if there are any signs that would link Marcus to this."

"I didn't notice anything when I ran in there," Jimmy said.

"Just go," Henry said.

Jimmy's upper lip twitched, but he obeyed his alpha's command.

"How long was he there?" I asked, unable to contain the morbid curiosity. Wolf blood wasn't enough to kill a vampire, especially not when used externally. "Did he die from blood loss? I didn't know that was even possible."

"It takes months," Ryder said. "He's probably been here a long time."

"How long has Marcus been missing?" I asked. "Two months? Longer?"

"He paid three months ago, but missed the last two." Henry's brow furrowed. "I don't know if I saw him during that time."

"Who do the cars belong to? Maybe they know something." The fact that two customer's cars were in the garage for months without anyone asking showed how rarely they were used as transportation. Though I supposed they could belong to Marcus.

"Good thinking." Derek rose and walked to the cars. He climbed in and began looking around.

"Help me get him out of here. We'll take him to the back and bury him. Let the bugs do the rest," Henry said.

I wrinkled my nose at the sight of the vampire being dragged across the cement floor. Stepping back from the garage, I spun around and nearly ran right into someone.

"Oh, sorry," I said, on impulse.

The dark-haired stranger looked down at me, his liquid silver eyes holding me captive. He smirked. "Hello, Isla."

My blood ran cold. He was even more handsome without the half mask covering his face and my cheeks flushed, as if remembering the way his body felt against mine.

A thud sounded behind me, followed by shoes crunching across gravel. "I didn't realize there were any day walking vampires in town," Henry said with a growl.

Vampire. My eyes widened and my pulse quickened as I took in the stranger. He was a vampire. Of all the supernaturals in Lost Harbor, the Crescent Pack hated vampires the most. So much so that there were laws forbidding relations with them.

Fuck me. By hooking up with him, I had literally

committed treason. If anyone found out, they could kill me.

"You're a vampire?" I whispered.

"I tried to warn you," he said.

"Your kind isn't allowed in our territory," Henry said. "You should go."

"Then how do you explain the dead one you were trying to hide?" the vampire asked with cool indifference.

"I don't think that's any of your business. You know the treaty. If a vampire comes into a shifter territory and poses a threat, we can take matters into our own hands." Henry cracked his knuckles and tilted his head to each side.

The vampire chuckled, and my eyes shot to him. He showed no signs of being intimidated by the fact that four large shifters were staring him down, as if he were a punching bag.

We all knew vampires were dangerous, and I'd only interacted with a few of them in my entire life. But this was the first time I had seen a vampire out in the sunlight without a trail of smoke following in his wake. The older the vampire, the stronger they were. I had heard stories that some could fully walk in the sun, but there hadn't been a vampire like that in this town for centuries. Who was this dude?

"Isla, back away. We can handle this," Ryder said.

My gaze was still fixed on the ridiculously attractive vampire. Only now I was glaring at him and my hands curled into fists. He knew how much trouble I would be in if any of them found out that I had sex with him. I was Crescent Pack property. I wasn't allowed to mingle with other supernatural species, and a dalliance with a vampire could literally lead to my death. I did not need this the same day that Ryder told me it was open season on me.

"Isla. Step back." Ryder's voice was laced with command, aggressive and controlling. A tone he rarely used with me.

I obeyed, not for fear of the vampire, but for fear of what would happen to me if the alpha and his friends found out what I had done with this particular vampire.

"I'm guessing he's the ex-boyfriend?" the vampire asked, a touch of amusement in his tone.

"What's that supposed to mean?" Ryder said. I felt his hand clamp around my forearm before he yanked me back, stepping between me and the threat.

"Someone very rudely left her tied up at a party where anyone could have found her," the vampire said smoothly.

I winced. Rider glanced at me, pure rage burning in his eyes. His look flipped a switch inside me. This was all his fault. I never would have met the vampire if I hadn't been left in that room, unable to escape.

"I told you to fucking untie me." I wasn't sure where the defiance had come from, but if I was going to be punished for my crime, I wanted Ryder to know the part he played in it.

"Don't look so scandalized. I was a gentleman. Mostly," the vampire took a step forward. "She was screaming so loudly I could hear her from outside the house. What was I supposed to do? The human part of me can't ignore a damsel in distress."

My eyes snapped to the vampire at the comment, and I scowled. I hated that he'd had to rescue me and that I'd let myself get into a position where I was helpless.

His expression softened for just a second and he offered a genuine smile. Then the glare returned, along with gritted teeth, as he turned back to the shifters. "What kind of male leaves a woman tied up and alone?"

Ryder surged forward, and the vampire met him in a blur so fast I couldn't track the movement. I wasn't even sure how it happened, but Ryder was on the ground and the vampire's foot was on his chest.

Henry and Derek took a step forward, but the vampire shook his head. "Careful now. You don't want to see what happens if you make me angry."

The shifters stopped. Henry growled. "Release my son."

"Your son needs to learn some manners," the vampire said.

To my surprise, Henry and Derek held their ground, neither shifter moving. Nostrils flaring, jaws clenched, they watched the vampire. And they waited.

There was absolutely nothing human about this creature. He couldn't blend in if he tried. Everything about him was more luminous than a human should be. He was too beautiful, too graceful, too... everything.

The heat that had been in my cheeks was spreading to the rest of my traitorous body. You would think I would have learned my lesson, but there was something so alluring about him. I could almost feel him calling to some buried darkness inside me. My body reacted instinctually, against my better judgment. I really hoped Ryder was too distracted to notice the rising arousal. I wanted to shut it down, regain control of my own senses, but it was a losing battle.

Based on the smirk on the vampire's face and the fact that his eyes raked up and down my body, I knew he hadn't missed a beat. He knew exactly how I was feeling. I hated him for it. I hated that he'd tricked me and that I enjoyed it. I hated that I wanted more.

His eyes left mine, and he looked down at Ryder, who was still under his foot. "If you're worried about her virtue, I didn't fuck her in the coat checkroom," he said. "I do wonder why someone would leave a naked woman tied up and vulnerable in a position where anyone could have abused her. That says far more about you than it does about me." He removed his foot from Ryder. "Now, play nice or I'll have to tear all of your heads off."

Henry stepped forward again but didn't charge the vampire as Ryder had. "This is your last warning. Leave our territory or we will make you."

The vampire brushed invisible dust from his shoulder before lifting his eyes to Henry. "That's where you're mistaken, my friend. All this territory is mine. The treaty doesn't apply to royals."

"There hasn't been a royal here in centuries," Henry

spat. "And I'm not about to start bowing down to some false royal now. Get the fuck out."

Another blur and the sound of bones cracking was only silenced when the screaming replaced it. My eyes widened as I watched all four shifters hit the ground, groaning in pain. When I caught sight of their mangled and broken limbs, I had to turn away. I'd kept the nausea at bay until then, but couldn't hold it back this time. After I emptied my guts, I turned back to the fallen shifters. Ryder was pushing himself up, hissing in pain as his right arm flopped, the bones in his forearm having been snapped in two.

Henry's shoulder was dislocated, and Derek's hands were facing the wrong direction. Jimmy's leg was bent in at an angle that shouldn't be possible. I closed my eyes for a moment, trying to comprehend the amount of power that had just been unleashed. He moved so fast I didn't even see it happen, yet he'd managed to inflict that much damage.

With the groans and cries of the shifters behind me, I focused on the vicious vampire in front of me. "Who are you?" I asked.

"To that group of assholes back there, I'm the king. But you can call me Dante," he winked.

I shook my head. "You should leave. I don't want anything to do with you."

"The wetness between your thighs says otherwise," he said. "Next time I see you, you'll be begging for my cock, Love."

# ELEVEN

Isla

TWO VAMPIRES SHOWED up at the Crescent Pack House the next morning. Both of them easily walking past sunny windows. They had to be just as ancient as the king and likely just as deadly. I kept a wide berth whenever we crossed paths, but they didn't seem to even notice me. Which was probably a good thing. They weren't here for me. They were here to observe the pack, by order of the vampire king.

It turns out, Lost Harbor used to be ruled by a royal vampire family. But they'd left town two-hundred years ago. The last royal had created the council as a temporary way to run the city until he could return.

None of the shifters had been alive when the king was

here, but most of the vampires and all the fae remembered. They had welcomed the king back with open arms.

Without the support of the vampires and fae, there would be no overthrowing the returned king. At least that's what I overheard when I got coffee that morning.

It seemed most of the pack was hoping his visit would be short lived and that things would go back to the way they were soon.

Henry was furious, which meant he had no time or energy for me. I had to admit, I was enjoying the chaos the vampires were causing. As a human, I wasn't a concern. They wouldn't bother me, but they sure as hell bothered Henry.

The pack was a buzz of activity, whispers in corners, and meetings behind locked doors. I was grateful for the solitude of my office. It was a little room that used to hold cleaning supplies. It was smaller than my old office, but it had a large window. My old office was in the basement, where it was always dark.

Thanks to the window, I'd been able to cover every solid surface with thriving plant life. It was almost like working inside my own personal garden. Just me and a shit ton of plants. Despite the fact that I wasn't thrilled about my life with the Crescent Pack, my little office was one of my favorite places in the world.

Though my bedroom and apartment were full of plants, they weren't nearly as lush as the greenery here. I think it was because I had all day to dote on them. I was one of those people who believed that plants thrived when you talked to them. Being the only human working in the heart of the pack, I was usually ignored. Which meant I spent more time than I'd like to admit talking to my plants. With the excitement of the vampire king's return, I'd be even less important.

It was nice knowing I could get my work done without interruption. Especially after Ryder's threat about not protecting me. There were much larger things to worry about than the future alpha's ex.

When I grabbed another cup of coffee in the kitchen, nobody even glanced my way. I caught whispers of conversation between Derek and Killian Moore, the pack's beta. At least Derek's hands were healed. The vampire king would have known that the injuries he caused would heal within a few hours. He wasn't trying to cause actual damage; he was making a point.

The memories of the screams and groans of pain flashed through my mind and I squeezed my eyes shut. I might hate how the pack treated us humans, but I didn't like seeing anyone in pain.

*Dante*. That was his name. What he'd asked me to call him. I shuddered. It felt too personal. Even though he'd been inside me, I wasn't about to get to know him better. He warned me how dangerous he was, and I didn't listen.

I added a sugar and cream to my coffee, stirring quietly while Derek and Killian whispered. There was nothing quiet about shifters. I was pretty sure they didn't have a low volume button. Even with my normal human hearing, I could make out every word.

"There hasn't been a royal here in two-hundred years," Derek said. "He must have found out."

"I thought you said it was taken care of," Killian hissed. "That nobody knew."

"Nobody should know," Derek said. "We covered our tracks."

"We've got a mole," Killian said.

I sipped my coffee, then tossed the stir stick in the trash can. Something big was going down, but my first thoughts weren't to find out more. Honestly, it only solidified my decision to leave this place.

Maybe I'd get lucky and the drama from the king's return would keep them off my back till the solstice.

As soon as I returned to my office, I picked up my phone and sent a quick text. *Can I send my final payment today?*

I had planned on waiting to send the last of the money, but I had enough if I basically drained my savings. I'd get paid a few more times before the solstice, and I was careful about what I spent. I'd feel better once it was done. No point in waiting.

The response came quickly. *Yes.*

I knew what he'd say, but I needed to see the confirmation, so I texted again. *Then I'm guaranteed a place, right?*

I watched the three little dots on the screen. When the

reply appeared, I let loose the breath I was holding. *Yes, I've held your spot. You're all good.*

Escaping from Lost Harbor was an ordeal in itself. I'd scheduled my departure with a smuggler a full year ago. It had felt so far away then, but it was nearly time. Knowing I only had to wait two more months made it so much easier to shut everything else out. Vampire royals back in town? Not my fucking problem.

My office door was ajar, and I knew I'd closed it when I left. With a sigh, I braced myself for an unwelcome visitor. Probably Ryder. It had been a nearly perfect morning alone in my office, but the silence was too good to last.

I took another sip of coffee to steady my nerves before pushing open the door the rest of the way. Surprisingly, my office was empty. I scanned the room, then checked behind the door just to be sure. Maybe I had left it open.

Then I noticed the big ass vase full of red roses on my desk. I'd been so preoccupied with looking for an intruder that I'd missed them on first inspection. Humans really were less observant than supernaturals. I rolled my eyes, already annoyed by whatever bullshit was bound to be on the card.

Ryder had never once sent me flowers while we'd been together, and after his performance yesterday, I thought he was finally over me. I set my mug on my desk and pulled the card off its plastic holder. My name was written in elegant script on the front of a tiny envelope.

Hesitating, I considered just throwing the whole thing in the trash, but I loved flowers and I couldn't bring myself to do it. Ryder must be beyond desperate. He'd been inside my apartment and my office a million times and he knew how much I loved plants. Yet, he'd never bothered with anything thoughtful like this. It was far too little too late. But I'd still keep the flowers.

I set the card down, still enclosed in the envelope, and moved the flowers to the side so they could stay on my desk while I worked. No reason to waste perfectly good roses.

When I left work at the end of the day, I considered taking the flowers home so I could pretend I threw them out. With my luck, I'd run into Ryder and he'd see me carting them home and read far too much into it. Plus, I'd have to answer Maddie's questions. I wasn't in the mood.

I'd worked late after getting behind with yesterday's excitement. The house was quiet. Most of the shifter's probably already gone. Or they'd gone off to do something about the dead vampire.

I shuddered at the memory of the vampire's emaciated body and pushed the thought away. No more. It was time to leave here and go home. Where there were no vampires and the only shifter was my best friend.

*Home.* Where a bottle of wine and my bathtub would make everything better.

My heart practically leaped out of my chest when I opened my door to find one of the visiting vampires waiting in the hallway. She was casually leaning against the wall as if she'd been there a while, but straightened when she saw me.

"Shit!" I exclaimed, placing my hand over my racing heart. "Are you trying to kill me?"

She cocked her head like a cat, and the corner of her mouth turned upward. Her gray eyes were lined with expertly applied eyeliner, accentuating her feline qualities. I hadn't seen the vampires up close and had avoided them all day, and I was surprised to see that she was smaller than me.

At five-foot-six, I was tiny compared to the shifters, but I was taller than many other human women. This vampire was petite. Almost fragile looking. She was nearly a head shorter than me, with a thin build. The oversized tee she wore over her leggings looked like it might swallow her whole.

"I've been waiting for your answer for hours." Her tone was bored and a little whiny.

"You must be looking for someone else," I said. "Want me to show you where Henry's office is?"

She chuckled. "I'm not on alpha duty. That's Luke's job. I'm here to watch over you."

"I'm sorry, what?"

"The king wants to know your answer." She sighed, not hiding her annoyance.

"I have no idea what you're talking about," I said. "Sorry I can't help." I walked forward, hoping she'd find something else to occupy her time if I just left.

"Did you get the flowers?"

I froze.

"Ah, you did. But you didn't read the card. I told him it was stupid and archaic and that girls didn't like flowers anymore. He never listens," she said. "I told him to send you the head of your ex-boyfriend. Now, that's a gift a girl can appreciate."

I spun to face her. "No, flowers are good. I love flowers."

She looked disappointed. "You sure you don't want me to take off his head? I'd be happy to oblige. Can even make look like an accident."

"No, thank you." I was furious with Ryder, but I didn't want him decapitated. Or maybe I did. Shit. What was wrong with me? Of course, I didn't want him dead. Guilt squeezed around my chest, and the vampire grinned.

"Interesting. So there is a dark side to you," she purred.

"I don't know what you're talking about," I hissed.

She shrugged. "Will you just read them damn note so I can give him your answer? I'm getting very, very hungry and we're not allowed to eat any of you."

I bristled, and a shiver ran down my spine. Well, that was good to know. But I didn't want to see what happened if I made a hungry vampire wait longer.

Quickly, I went back to my office and retrieved the abandoned envelope. Inside was a simple white card with one sentence. It wasn't a question. It was a command. If I were a wolf shifter, I'd be growling. As it was, I bared my teeth in response to the presumptuous statement. *Go to dinner with me.*

"Well?" the vampire asked.

"It isn't exactly a question," I grumbled.

"So, yes?"

"Um, fuck no. I'm not having dinner with him. You do realize what happens to humans who mingle with species outside their bonds?" I asked.

"Should I?"

"They'd kill me if I got close to him," I said.

"Didn't you *already* get close to him?" She lifted a sculpted brow.

"Of course not," I said. *Lies, all lies.* But I wasn't about to tell her what happened.

She scoffed. "Whatever. Not my problem. Nine-hundred years and he still has me doing stupid errands."

"He's nine-hundred years old?" I asked.

"Oh, no, sweetie. That's how long I've known him. He's far older than that. And just to warn you, he's not going to ask nicely again," she said.

"That was nice?" I pointed to the card.

"That was fucking poetry," she said.

I crossed my arms over my chest. "I don't care how old he is. I don't want anything to do with him. This isn't some teen romance story where the human girl gets all swept away by the broody vampire. In case you didn't notice, I deal with enough monsters as it is. I don't need another one."

"I'll let him know," she said.

Then she vanished. No blur, not so much as a breeze. She just vanished.

I swallowed hard. I super fucked up when I hooked up

with him in the closet. He tried to warn me, but I didn't listen.

Even though it hurt, I dumped the roses in the trash can. I couldn't have anyone asking me where they'd come from tomorrow. Thankfully, the evening custodian was a human who would keep her mouth shut.

# TWELVE

Isla

THEY FOUND two more dead vampires. Drained of their blood and left in abandoned buildings near the docks. Two more vampires showed up at the Crescent Pack house, and I had never seen Henry this flustered. We had four vampires stalking our halls and watching our every move. Even I was unnerved by their presence.

When he stopped in my office, our conversations were tense and quick. Just the information I needed to add to the expense reports and nothing more. All the gossip came from the other humans in the house.

Typically, I avoided the common areas, but with four lethal vampires walking around, my office didn't feel as safe as it used to.

The kitchen was usually hit or miss in terms of interacting with the few other humans who worked in the mansion. The last three days have been packed every time I ventured out. I wasn't the only one waiting to hear updates.

"Hey, Viki," I called as I set my mug on the counter in front of the coffeepot.

The older human woman looked up. "Oh, hey, Isla." Then she returned to staring at the wall in front of her.

I carried my cup to the table and sat down in the chair across from her.

Viki's gray dress and apron, which were usually meticulous, were wrinkled and something red was smeared on the apron. I tried not to think too hard about what it was, even though I knew that color well. Her gray hair was a frizzy mess, her usual neat braid nearly unraveled. Something bad had happened. "You okay?"

She didn't take her eyes off the wall. "They found another one."

My brows lifted. "Another vampire?"

She nodded slowly. "This one wasn't fully dead."

"Viki, what happened?" I set my hand on hers, hoping to bring her some comfort.

She looked at me again, her expression hollow and empty. "He was still alive, but we didn't know. We just tried to take him down. We thought he'd be dead like the others and we didn't want to leave him like that..."

I waited, my brow furrowing.

"I don't think it was on purpose, you know. He'd been

starving. There for days, at least." She shook her head. "Lucy never had a chance."

A lump rose in my throat. Lucy was new here. Sixteen years old and like me and Viki, she'd chosen not to go the route of using her body as currency. She'd been assigned here to the housekeeping staff. She had an innocence few here had. I didn't think she'd last long, but I figured it would be because she got swept up in some shifter's false promises.

"He didn't stop. There was so much blood." Viki went back to staring at the wall.

"I'm so sorry," I said.

"I tried." She let out a choked cry. "I tried to stop him. But he was too strong. They're monsters. All of them. We were helping."

I squeezed her hand. "Is there someone who can take you home?"

"I have to finish my work," she said.

"No, you don't," I said. "I'll take care of it. You should go home. Get cleaned up."

"They staked him in front of me. They still killed him. Lucy's death was for nothing," she said.

"You know the rules," I said, not sure why I was saying it. "I'm sure they didn't mean any disrespect toward Lucy."

"Yeah." She opened her mouth as if to say more, then her eyes widened in terror at something behind me.

I turned to see all four vampire visitors standing in the kitchen. "Not a good time," I snapped.

The female I'd talked to a few days ago titled her head to the side. "Your alpha has given us permission to go anywhere we please."

"Well, I'm telling you to get the fuck out. You don't need to be in a kitchen, anyway," I snapped.

Viki's grip tightened around mine, her fingernails biting into my hand. I clenched my jaw, keeping my gaze on the vampires. The petite female I'd already interacted with was the smallest of the four. The other three were large males who looked every inch the security guards or jailers they felt like.

"There was a dead vampire in the Crescent Pack house, which means our killer is probably here. And you're speaking to me this way?" She seemed amused.

"We both know I don't have the strength to capture a vampire. And neither does my human friend here, who is terrified right now. So, get. The fuck. Out."

"Interesting," one of the males said. "She's not afraid of us."

I glared at him. Daring him to challenge me. Humans had it hard enough as it was in this pack. I wasn't about to let outsiders make it worse.

"Let's go," the female said.

As soon as they were out of sight, my shoulders sagged and I let out a breath. My hands shook.

"You were scared," Viki said.

"Of course I was," I said. "But that doesn't mean we can't stand up for ourselves."

"I wish they'd just leave us alone," she said.

"I know, but until they figure out who has been killing these vampires, we're stuck with them," I said.

"Do you think she's right? That it's someone in the pack?" Viki asked.

"Where did you find the vampire?" I asked gently.

"In the shed outside, where we keep the gardening tools. We hardly ever go in there," she said. "But the gardening crew had to cancel this week, so they asked us to weed the flower beds."

There were better places to hide a body in the Crescent Pack mansion. I frowned, considering her question. "I don't think so. It's outside the mansion; anyone who got into the grounds could access it. If it was someone here, there are better places to hide a vampire's body."

"Yeah, maybe you're right," she said.

"Hopefully, they figure out who's doing this soon and deal with them so we can all just move on," I said.

It took me a few more minutes to convince her to go home and get some rest. I left the kitchen feeling more uneasy. The bodies were getting more frequent and closer to home. Hiding them in abandoned buildings was one thing, but to put one in the shed outside the pack house felt like a message. Who would be that stupid to risk being caught by the pack?

Unless the killer was someone in the inner circle. I was thinking it even when I assured Viki it wasn't possible. I just didn't want to scare her. At this point, the killer could be anyone. Maybe it wasn't even a shifter at all. Maybe it was a vampire who was using our territory as a dumping ground.

The sooner they figured this out, the better.

I set my keys on the kitchen counter and went right for a drink. Every day at work felt intense now. Everyone was on edge and it was as if the tension was in the very air we breathed.

A nearly dead plant was sitting next to the bourbon bottle, a note in front of it. *I think I killed it. I shouldn't be trusted with plants.*

I smiled at Maddie's note. She had started taking an interest in plants after we moved in together and had several in her bedroom, but every so often, she would leave a plant out for me to fix. I touched the brittle brown leaves. I was pretty sure it was dead, but I liked a good challenge.

Working in the dirt helped me feel more calm, more centered and connected. I clipped off the dead leaves and watered the plant, hoping I could nurse it back to life. I'd brought back a few plants I thought were dead before. It was worth trying.

When I finished with the possibly dead plant, I watered the rest of the plants around our apartment and then stripped to shower. I rarely had plans, but tonight I was heading out.

Thankfully, there were no shifters or vampires where I was going. After the last few days, the quiet and space was needed, now more than ever.

# THIRTEEN

Isla

EACH YEAR, on the anniversary of my grandmother's death, I visited her grave after sunset.

My grandmother had shared my affinity for plants and had taught me how to care for them. She'd passed when I was ten. That was before my life went to absolute shit. My mom had always been a loose cannon, but I could count on the peace my grandmother's greenhouse brought. After she passed, I started visiting her grave often, but it was too hard to go all the time.

Now, I used the anniversary of her death as a marker for when I needed to resume care for the flowers I'd planted over the years. Most were dormant in the winter and now that it was spring, there were lovely green shoots and signs of life. It made me feel better to see the rebirth of nature in this place of death.

I only visited at night anymore. It was when the devil's trumpets, her favorite flower, bloomed. She'd kept an entire corner of her greenhouse to grow them year round. Now, I only saw them in the warmer months.

The ancient, crumbling cemetery had scared me when I was a kid, but now it was a place of solace. When I'd go in the day, I'd sometimes run into other people. Sometimes even funerals in progress. At night, it was me and the owls. It was better this way.

I grabbed the little allium starters to add to the garden around my grandmother's headstone. I was hoping they were hardy enough to thrive without me, since I'd only be here to care for them for one summer. Each year, I added more plants, and the place was starting to look a little wild. My grandmother would have approved.

Cool spring air bit through my hoodie, but the brisk walk warmed me up quickly. The cemetery was only a mile away, and the walk warmed me enough that I was a little sweaty by the time I arrived.

Wind rustled through the trees and something skittered across the grounds as I approached the iron gate. Crescent Pack territory had two cemeteries. One for shifters, one for everyone else. This one was mostly humans but some of the older headstones belonged to other species from hundreds of years ago. This cemetery was at the end of our territory. The other side was vampire lands.

I used to worry that I'd cross the nocturnal creatures, but they had little use for a cemetery. I was pretty sure they didn't bother with burying the humans they overfed from. It was illegal for them to kill their food, but we all knew that accidents happened. Not that they'd tell anyone when they did. The iron gate groaned as I pushed it open. The half-moon illuminated the gravel path enough that I could make my way through despite my poor human vision. I noticed a mound of fresh dirt with a wood marker stuck in front of it, and I wondered if it belonged to Lucy. It would take a while for the headstone to come in. I made note to come back in a couple of weeks to plant some flowers around her grave. She had her whole life ahead of her. She shouldn't be six feet under. Another human lost to the monsters of this city.

I moved forward, noting the few headstones with faded stuffed animals or dead flowers. None of the graves had any new or fresh offerings. People didn't make it out here often, myself included. I knew I couldn't linger on the fact that my grandmother was here. It created a connection to this place, brought back happy memories. If she was still alive, I might not have the strength to leave. I'd have stayed for her. Besides, she'd have the company of the plants I left for her once I was gone.

Somehow, my grandmother had found a way to exist here, to thrive even. I never knew what she did to pay her bills, but she'd never pledged to any pack or supernatural group. She paid protection to the Crescent Pack, and they left her alone. That was all I knew.

When I'd asked my mom about it, she'd gone white and told me to be careful about digging up the past. If it was bad enough to freak out my mom, I wasn't sure I wanted to know. I needed to believe my grandmother was one of the good ones. There were so few innocent, kind people in this city. I needed to believe that at least one of the residents here had been good. Even if it was likely a lie.

The gravel path vanished, and I entered the older and less cared for part of the cemetery. The grass grew wild here; nobody cared for the plants or bothered to make a path. It was peaceful, even if it was a hodgepodge of random headstones, statues, and memorial benches. Some of the stone structures had been completely reclaimed by nature. They were so covered in vines and greenery that the names were long gone.

That was my hope for my grandmother's headstone. When I left, the flowers I planted would take over and she could become part of nature in a way.

Finally, I made my way to her headstone and smiled at the sight of the devil's trumpets spreading away from her grave. They'd surrounded several other headstones at this point, but nobody ever came to visit those. At least they got flowers this way. Sure, they were poisonous, but they were beautiful. A fitting tribute to the creatures that lurked in Lost Harbor. Often nice to look at, but dangerous nonetheless.

"Hey grams," I said as I tiptoed around the toxic flowers to find a clear area to plant. I dropped to my knees in a patch of grass. "How's eternity treating you?" I dug my fingers into the dirt, making a hole with my bare hands so I could plant the new flowers I'd brought. As I worked, I told my grandmother about my life this past year. Including my plan to leave. Saying it out loud was liberating. I hadn't told anyone yet, not even Maddie.

When I was finished planting, I leaned back on my feet and brushed my hands together to get off some of the dirt. "You know, I think you'd be proud of me for following my dreams." It was what she'd always told me to do. Which was what everyone told you when you were a kid, of course. But I think she'd really meant it. I closed my eyes and listened to the wind rustling the trees. This place had a sense of quiet you couldn't find anywhere else.

"Well, well, isn't this a surprise," a deep, rumbling voice cut through the silence.

My eyes popped open, and I fell to the side as I turned to see who'd joined me. "Seriously?"

Dante smirked. "I thought you'd be happy to see me."

"Why would you think that?" I got to my feet, then brushed the dirt off my jeans.

"We had a moment, in case you forgot," he said.

"You lied to me," I snapped.

"I never lied to you. I told you I was no good for you. You didn't heed my warning," he said.

"You were at a shifter party. You should have told me you're a vampire."

"I'm the king," he said. "I go where I please. These divisions between supernaturals didn't exist last time I was here."

"You've been gone a long time, then," I said.

"I have. Too long, by the looks of it," he said.

I ignored his comment and started walking, eager to get away from him. He grabbed my upper arm, his fingers digging into my flesh.

"Let go of me," I said.

"You ignored my dinner invitation," he said.

"That wasn't an invitation. It was a command. Nobody tells me what to do," I said.

"Oh, I think you'd rather enjoy it if I told you what to do," he said.

"Someone thinks rather highly of himself," I said. "The sex wasn't that good."

He pulled me toward him, then wrapped his arm around me so I was flush against him. I gasped, my body already heating, tension already curling low in my belly.

I sucked in a breath and backed away just enough to test him. He loosened his grip. If I wanted to leave, he'd let me. So why did I stay?

"You can't make a comment like that and then not expect me to take it as a challenge." With an arm still wrapped around me, his other hand released my arm and his large palm swept up from my hip, dipping under my tee. I sucked in a breath as his deft fingers trailed up my stomach, over my ribs until they reached the underwire of my bra. He pushed the flimsy fabric aside, freeing my breasts. My nipples tightened and my breathing quickened. I should say something, I should stop him. I knew he would if I said the word, but I couldn't find the willpower to make him stop.

I didn't want him to stop.

"We shouldn't," I said.

His hand stilled. "Do you want me to let you go? I'll walk away right now if that's your desire."

Those silver eyes were like molten steel, pulling me in to their depths. I stared at him, willing the words to come. I knew the risk of staying, but I didn't want to leave.

"The choice is always yours," he said.

"Don't stop," I breathed out.

He licked his lower lip, and I caught sight of those fangs. His hand kneaded and caressed each breast, then his mouth was on my neck. Kissing, licking... sharp teeth scraped against the sensitive flesh and a thrill of both desire and fear flared and I pulled away. "No. You can't bite me."

"I won't bite you, Love," he said. "But I do want to taste you."

He scooped me up and carried me a few steps, then dropped me at the base of a marble statue of an angel. Gently, he pushed me against the cool stone before dropping to his knees in front of me. My breath hitched at the sight of the vampire king kneeling before me. A heady rush of power welled up, making my chest expand. He didn't seem like the kind of male who would ever get on his knees for anyone.

"Do you taste as sweet as you smell?" He asked as he

slowly unbuttoned my jeans. My breath was coming out in heavy pants and hadn't even touched me yet.

Hearing those words from a vampire sent a thrill of fear mixed with anticipation. He said he wouldn't bite me, but I hardly knew him. For a moment, I wondered if I should ask him to stop. Did I really want this? Again?

I did.

His thumbs hooked under my waistband, and he paused as if waiting for me to object. Instead, I gripped his shoulders to steady myself. I caught a wicked gleam in his eyes before he lowered my pants. I felt like I was living someone else's life; someone who was sexier and more self-assured than me. It was one thing to tease Ryder, but this was new territory. I'd only ever been with clumsy shifters or humans as a teen, and then there was Ryder.

Dante was something else.

I'd had a taste before, but we'd been rushed and caught up in the moment. This felt different. More intimate. It was everything I tried to avoid by keeping people at arm's length. Yet, it didn't feel scary with him. It felt right.

My jeans were cast aside, landing on top of a random headstone. Completely bare from the waist down, I waited for the shame or fear to come.

It didn't.

I just wanted to feel good. I wanted to feel alive. For so long, I'd gone through the motions. Done as expected. This was the opposite of everything I was supposed to do.

If anyone found out about this, I'd be marked a traitor. I knew what I was risking, but I didn't care.

An owl swooped overhead, and the trees rustled in the breeze. If not for that, I might have feared that time had stood still. His touch on my thigh was reverent, gentle and tender. Nothing like I expected. Then he tightened his grip and lifted my thigh over his shoulder. I had to grip him tighter to maintain my balance and a pair of strong hands settled on my hips, holding me in place against the marble statue.

When his mouth found my center, there was nothing gentle about it. His tongue and teeth and lips were sinful perfection, and I gasped as the pleasure began to build. One of his hands moved from my hip, sliding around my ass. Then it was gone, and I only had a moment before he plunged a finger inside me. I moaned, my back arching as I succumbed to the pleasure. My knees felt weak, and I panted wantonly as he continued to thrust and lick. He added another finger, and I cried out as my climax neared.

It wasn't much longer before I was screaming, my body fully under his spell. The sculpture against my back was the only thing keeping me from collapsing to the ground. My fingernails bit into his shoulders hard enough to draw blood. He feasted on me, licking and sucking as I came over and over. Finally, he released me, and I leaned back as I worked to catch my breath.

Strong arms were around me in an instant, cradling me protectively to keep me from falling. I collected myself, then stepped away. As the fog of orgasm lifted, I realized the gravity of what I'd just done.

All those good thoughts. All that confidence melted away. I had a plan. I was leaving here. I needed to lay low, stay out of trouble, and bide my time.

This was the opposite of all that. Part of me wanted to yield to him completely, but if I did, I would stay. I hardly knew him, and I already knew that if I went any deeper, I would stay for him.

That wasn't right. This wasn't who I was. I was the least romantic person in the world. I didn't fall for my boyfriend of two years, let alone a stranger. One who was forbidden at that.

What the hell had I been thinking? I wasn't thinking. I was following my libido. Dammit. I was smarter than that.

"Shit. Shit. Shit." I tiptoed over to where my pants were and pulled them back on, not bothering to find my underwear. "We can't do this. I don't like you. You tricked me the other day, and you somehow did it again. I belong to the wolf pack. I can't do this with you."

He smirked, then stuck his fingers, the fingers that had been inside me, in his mouth and licked them clean one at a time.

I repressed a shiver and turned away from him. My body was craving more, but I couldn't give in. Instead, I went hunting for my shoes. I didn't even recall removing my shoes. How deep in the fog of lust had I been?

"I had no choice but to defend my honor," he said. "Have you changed your mind?"

I finished lacing up my shoes, then glared at him. "About what?"

"About the sex. You said it wasn't that good."

"I don't have enough information to make that kind of assessment," I said.

He barked out a laugh. "That sounds like another challenge."

"Absolutely not. I am not dying just so you can stroke your ego," I said.

"Oh, this has nothing to do with stroking my ego, but I'm more than happy to stroke other things," he said.

"Stay away from me," I said. "You're going to get me killed. If anyone had seen us..."

"Don't worry, Love, if anyone tries to hurt you, I'll kill them," he said matter-of-factly.

"I'm not asking you to do that. There's been enough death already as it is," I said darkly, thinking of Lucy.

"That's true, but I always protect what's mine," he said.

"I'm not yours," I snapped. I turned and started walking away, then glanced back. "Don't follow me."

# CHAPTER
# FOURTEEN

Isla

EVERY TIME I TURNED A CORNER, my pulse raced. I'd dreamed about Dante last night, and it was so real that I soaked my panties. I had never had a dream like that before. It was so twisted, feeling both turned on and disgusted. It made me question my own feelings. What was wrong with me if part of me wanted to be with him again? How had I let him seduce me so easily last night?

I knew there was more to it. I knew I was attracted to him. But I'd worked too hard to lose it all now. I had a plan. And a forbidden vampire boyfriend was not part of it. Especially not one as dangerous and powerful as him.

I turned another corner and ran right into someone. "Shit. Sorry."

As I regained my bearings, I realized the someone was the petite vampire female.

"Thoughts elsewhere?" she asked.

"I don't think my thoughts are your business," I said, hoping she wasn't one of the vampires we'd been told about who could read minds.

"I think we got off on the wrong foot," she said. "I'm Anna."

My eyes narrowed with suspicion. "You're here to see if you can get any dirt on my pack. What kind of *foot* do you think we could be on?"

She chuckled. "It's sweet how you call them your pack when you're nothing more than a pretty caged bird."

I bristled at the comment. It was true, but I hated being reminded of it. "You speak as if you know me. As if you know the choices I've had to make or what I've done to survive. You have no right to judge me."

She lifted a brow. "You're right. I don't know you." She inclined her head in a little bow. "Nice to see you again, Isla."

Then she walked away, her steps smooth and graceful. I watched her until she was out of sight. My brows pulled together as I tried to figure out her play. Was she hoping to get something out of me? Not that I knew anything, but why try to be nice? Our other interactions hadn't exactly been friendly.

It didn't matter. I had things to do. I'd sent the final payment to the smuggler already. Nearly every penny I had went to that bargain. There was no turning back now.

Things were moving right along and I was getting closer by the day to my exit from this place.

The Crescent Pack and the vampires weren't going to be my concern for much longer.

When I opened my office door, my heart sank. The interaction with Anna had been more than enough bull-shit for one day. I didn't need this.

Ignoring Ryder, where he sat in my chair behind my desk, I went to the tall filing cabinet and stuffed my purse in the bottom drawer behind the files. Then I turned to face the shifter. "What do you want?"

"That's a terrible greeting," he said.

"You stopped getting a nice greeting the day you told me you were going to let the pack go after me," I said.

"So dramatic," he said.

"Sure, I'm the dramatic one." I didn't hide the sarcasm.

"I came to check in on you," he said.

"Why?"

"Because you're still part of my pack. An important part. My dad says you're the best financial person we've ever had," he said.

"You'd think that would earn me something more than animosity and threats," I said.

"It's just how things are around here, you know that." He stood, then walked around the desk. "It's nothing personal."

"It feels personal when your dad slaps me across the

face as soon as you declare that you're no longer going to protect me," I said.

His expression darkened for a moment, and I saw a brief flash of gold in his eyes. It faded quickly, but it had been impossible to miss. He didn't know his dad hit me. And he didn't like it.

That was interesting.

I thought things between us were over a long time ago. He'd certainly moved on with plenty of other women, but now I knew he'd never gotten over me. He needed to, though. I didn't love him. It was almost enough to make me feel bad for him.

Guilt squeezed my chest, and I almost wanted to give him a hug. Almost.

"You can't do that," I said.

"Do what?" he asked.

"The possessive boyfriend bit. We're not a couple," I said.

"I know. I also know someone gave you flowers," he said. "I could buy you flowers."

My face heated. Dammit. Whoever had cleaned my office reported to him. I didn't realize he was keeping tabs on me that closely. "You never once bought me flowers."

"If that's what you need, I can make it happen," he said.

I lifted a brow at the choice of words. He would likely get one of the human servants to pick them up for me. One of the things I loved about plants was how personal they were. Flowers had meanings, plants served purposes. They brought something to the room and to the person caring for them. Plants were so much more than just cut flowers in a vase sent as a meaningless gesture. Much like the roses I'd tossed in the trash. Those were *thanks for the sex* roses.

"Ryder, I can't do this with you. Please, let me go," I said.

He moved closer to me, a low growl in his throat. "I keep trying to let you go, but you won't leave my head. It's as if you've possessed me, made it so I can't be with anyone else."

"That's just because you can't have me," I said. "The feeling will pass."

"I don't think so." He stopped inches from me. "Who is he? The new man?"

"I threw the roses in the trash," I pointed out. "Clearly, I'm not interested."

"That's what made me think I might have a shot," he said.

"You left me naked in a closet!" I stomped my foot on the floor, the anger surging without realization. I hadn't let myself dwell on how dangerous that situation had been. If anyone else had found me, so many awful things could have happened.

Ryder inched forward, and I backed up, trying to keep some distance between us. All too soon, I was against the wall and out of options. He continued forward, boxing me in with his arms.

"You drive me crazy, Isla," he said. "I thought if I got

one last taste, I could let you go. But our plans were interrupted."

"If you hadn't left me naked and tied up, I'd have found you later," I said.

"I was planning to come back for you," he said, his voice soft and soothing. He dropped one hand and brushed a loose strand of hair away from my face. "What do you say? Just one last fuck? Help me get you out of my head."

"Let me go," I said.

He leaned forward and kissed my jaw. I tensed, considering what would happen if I kicked him in the nuts and ran. I didn't think he'd force me, but he wasn't acting the same as he had when we were dating. If I attacked him, I was risking his wolf. I had to be smart about this. I didn't know this Ryder. He wasn't the same male I'd been with. Had his wolf changed him or was he always like this, but good at hiding it?

He inhaled, taking a deep breath. I shuddered. Fucking shifters and their obsession with scents.

His whole body tensed and he leaned back, palms against the wall, arms framing my head. "Why do you smell like a vampire?"

My pulse raced. "What? Why would I smell like a vampire?"

He sniffed again. "You reek of vampire."

"Well, we do have several blood suckers wandering around the house," I pointed out.

"No, I've smelled them. This is something different."

His brow furrowed and I could almost see him working out the connection.

Before I could think it through, I leaned forward and pressed my lips to his. He made a surprised sound and his lips didn't respond to mine. I reached down, cupping the bulge in his jeans.

He groaned, then pressed against me, his lips moving in time with mine. His hands moved to my face, holding me in place while his mouth assaulted mine; the kiss desperate, claiming, violent.

My body reacted to the feel of his against mine and I ground against him, moaning into the kiss. I shut off my mind, letting my instincts take over. This was just sex. And it was survival. Nobody could know what I did. And as Dante had pointed out, the best way to get a male's scent off you was to fuck another one.

"Just this once," I said, between kisses, my voice breathy.

"Just once," he agreed.

I could do this. It was sex. Besides, I was still reeling a bit from my dreams last night. I could use the release.

Ryder's hands began to work the button on my jeans, and I reached for his. I didn't want this, but I knew the consequences if anyone found out about Dante. Internally cursing him, I worked Ryder's pants free and reminded myself that this was just sex.

My body responded to every touch as calloused hands slid under my shirt, over my stomach, pausing at my breasts. Ryder pushed the bra up, his hands rough as he squeezed each breast; his thumb stroked each sensitive nipple, and they tightened under the attention. Breathing shallow, my hips seemed to move without instruction, desperate for friction.

"I knew there was a little whore in there," Ryder hissed.

The dirty word sent heat straight to my core. I should be insulted, but I liked it. I bit down on his lower lip and he growled. Suddenly, he pulled away, then shoved me toward my desk. Gripping my hair, he roughly pushed me down until I was bent over my desk, my ass in the air.

My eyes widened, and I grabbed hold of the edge of my desk as Ryder roughly pulled my pants down. I could feel his hard length against my bare ass. He leaned down, his body hard and heavy against me. Soft lips brushed against my neck and I moaned in anticipation.

Yanking on my hair hard, Ryder pulled my head back, so I was staring into his eyes. He had that wild golden gleam; his wolf was simmering below the surface. Fear curled in my chest, but the warning didn't win over my arousal.

He leaned down, his mouth sucking, licking, and kissing my neck. His warm breath lingered near my ear and he whispered, "This is just sex and I'm going to use you like a slut."

His cock slammed into me. I cried out, the initial thrust deep and hard and painful. I adjusted to the sensation and my breathing quickened as an orgasm built. I shouldn't like this. I shouldn't be getting off on this. But I was soaked, my juices dripping; my pussy tightening around him as each thrust brought new waves of pleasure.

My fingers tightened around the edge of my desk and I held on as he slammed into me. There was nothing sweet or considerate about his movements. He was pounding into me aggressively, violently.

His grip tightened on my hair, pulling my head back as he continued to impale me. Pain mingled with pleasure, making my back arch as I gasped for air.

Ryder's large hand wrapped around my throat possessively. The touch was gentle, a complete contrast to the feeling of his cock inside me and the pain of his other hand in my hair. "Come for me."

I cried out, pleasure exploding through me.

Ryder groaned, his cock twitching as he found his release.

Panting, I stayed where I was laying across my desk. A flicker of guilt danced through me, but I shoved it away. This was just sex. It didn't mean anything. I was allowed to enjoy sex. Even if it was with Ryder.

He gently caressed my throat, then moved his hand to my chin, turning my face so I was looking at him. "Damn, Isla. You are such a good little slut." He pulled out of me.

His filthy words made me feel like I was on fire, but I wasn't about to let him know that. I stood and watched him dress, cum dripping down my thighs. "Too bad it's the last time this is going to happen."

He stepped closer to me, then traced my lower lip with his index finger. "We'll see about that."

My whole body was still feeling the aftershocks of the orgasm when he walked out of my office.

I knew I couldn't do that again. Ryder and I had too much history. But damn, where was that heat when we'd been together? Everything with us had been so gentle and sweet. I never knew sex could be like that. It really was too bad it was the last time. Ryder wasn't who I wanted to be with. Even if that sex had been spectacular. Though it had never been like that before. I wondered who he'd been with to learn his new skills.

Once again, I realized that the thought of him with someone else didn't even send the tiniest flicker of jealousy.

I wanted to be with someone I loved so deeply that the thought of sharing them made my soul cleave in two. Maybe that was stupid, or maybe my standards were too high. The only thing I knew for certain was that Ryder wasn't that person for me.

# CHAPTER
# FIFTEEN

Isla

My apartment was dark when I arrived home and I flipped on the light to find Maddie and her girlfriend making out, half-naked, on the couch. Maddie shoved Kaylie off and grabbed a blanket to cover them.

I looked away. "Oh, shit, sorry."

"Hey, Isla. I thought you were working late tonight."

"It's seven," I said, risking a glance back.

"Wow, I totally lost track of time!" Maddie said.

They were both wrapped up in the same blanket, and Kaylie's cheeks were bright pink. "Hey, Isla. Nice to see you again."

"So, you two are back together?" I wasn't sure I agreed with it. How many times was Maddie going to have her heart broken?

"For good, this time," Maddie said.

Kaylie brushed a loose strand of hair away from Maddie's face and stared at her with such admiration I almost forgot about all the heartbreak she'd caused. She looked up at me. "I learned my lesson. Maddie was kind enough to give me another chance."

"A last chance, I hope," I said, coming across harsher than I expected.

"Isla!" Maddie hissed.

"No, I deserve that," Kaylie said. "I know I caused her pain, and I will never do that again. I know you were the one who had to help her pick up the pieces when it should be me who's there to support her."

I didn't hide the doubt in my expression, but I really did want Maddie to find happiness. My shoulders slumped and I let out a sigh, telling myself that this was Maddie's choice. Fixing a smile on my face, I nodded at Kaylie. "I'm happy for both of you."

Maddie planted a kiss on her girlfriend's cheek. "Should we take this to my room?"

"Or my place?" Kaylie proposed. "I do live alone. We can make all the noise we want."

Maddie giggled. "I like the sound of that."

Neither of them seemed to be aware of my presence in the room anymore and I suddenly felt like I was watching something I shouldn't be seeing. This was their reunion, and it was between them. Quietly, I walked through the room to my door. It squeaked when I opened it and I winced, hating that I was intruding on their moment.

"Night, Isla," Maddie called.

I turned back to the couple on the couch. "Night. And congratulations."

They both beamed at me, and I slipped into my room to give them some privacy. About ten minutes later, I heard the sound of the front door close and my phone buzzed.

I glanced at the text from Maddie. *See you tomorrow.*

At least one of us found love. Maddie deserved it and I was happy for her, but seeing her happily reunited with her ex made me feel a little unbalanced about what I'd done today. I needed a shower. I couldn't smell him on me the way supernaturals could, but I suddenly had the overwhelming desire to get his scent off me.

I scrubbed my skin till it was pink, hoping that the interlude with Ryder was enough to hide the scent of vampire. I'd gone from a six-month drought to hooking up with two different males. My teen years had been full of disappointing experiences with a few males who didn't know their way around a female body. Once I found Ryder, there was nobody else. Until that closet with the vampire king. I shook my head. How had I gotten to this point? I enjoyed sex, but there was too much attachment that went along with it.

Sometimes, I envied the girls who were so open with their sexuality. I loved sex and I enjoyed it. I'd grown up in a home where sex was currency, but it was also intimacy. It let people get too close and it caused you to show vulnerabilities. I couldn't afford that.

Someone was pounding on my door, and I was dripping wet from my shower. Tugging the towel around me, I left my bathroom without bothering to dry my hair. Had Kaylie already fucked things up with Maddie?

Blowing out a breath, I tried to send the tightness from my jaw. Screaming about how awful Kaylie was wouldn't help Maddie. If she was back already, she'd need a shoulder to cry on, not a lecture. Unless Kaylie followed her here. Then I was prepared to chase her away from our apartment for hurting my best friend.

I was prepared to comfort Maddie or scream at her girlfriend. I was not prepared for opening my door to find a smoking hot vampire smirking at me.

"Mother fucker," I said through gritted teeth.

"It's nice to see you again, Love." His eyebrows lifted as he took me in, seemingly enjoying that I was soaking wet and only in a towel.

I glared at him. "What are you doing here?"

He grinned, showing straight white teeth. I knew there were fangs in there too, but they weren't extended right now.

My nipples tightened at the memory of those fangs grazing my skin. I tried to tell myself I was responding to the cold and not his presence, but something about him seemed to call to me. He was literally like poison. Hooking up with him again could kill me.

"I have to say, you look amazing with wet hair," he said. There was that accent again, something that I couldn't quite place. That had to be why every word seemed to drip with seduction. I was a sucker for an accent.

"You can't be here," I said. "This is shifter territory."

"All of Lost Harbor is my territory," he said. "As you already know."

"Am I supposed to be impressed by that?" I asked.

"Most women are," he said. "I am a king."

"We haven't had a king here in centuries. Nobody even knows who you are or why you left. My whole life it's just been the council running things. To me, this is their town," I said.

He winced dramatically and set his hand on his heart. "Ouch. You take a vacation and everyone forgets all about you."

"Two hundred years is not a vacation," I said.

He shrugged. "Time starts to lose meaning after a while."

"Not for us humans," I said. "Who, I might need to remind you, are mortal."

He leaned against the wall near my doorbell. "I think that's one of the reasons I find you so appealing. Usually, I can't stand humans. I've certainly never shown up at a woman's doorstep before."

"You need to leave," I said, ignoring the flip of my stomach at his words. Those silver eyes felt like they were peering into my soul. I knew if I didn't send him packing now, I was going to make another mistake.

And there was no way in hell I was going to fuck Ryder again. That could not happen.

"I know you don't want me to leave. I can smell your pussy from here. You're already wet thinking about me," he said.

Holy ever-loving fuck. He was right, of course. And his words made my core clench in anticipation. The memory of his mouth against my clit sent a surge of heat through me, and I had to resist the urge to drop my towel and invite him in.

I remembered how good sex was with him in that closet. What would it be like to take our time? To leave the lights on and explore each other's bodies before taking him in my mouth and making him feel as good as he'd made me feel.

"No." The word startled me. I hadn't meant to say it out loud. Quickly, I forced a stern expression on my face. "I don't want you and you can't be here."

"Your body betrays your mouth," he said, then he leaned forward, mere inches separating us. "Oh, the things I could do with that mouth of yours. To feel it wrapped around my cock..."

My eyes widened, and it felt like my whole body was on fire. I had always enjoyed sex, but I never craved it before. Not like this. Not like how I wanted it with him. "You have no idea what I had to do after our last encounter."

"I can smell him on you." His upper lip twitched and his silver eyes darkened for a moment. "I hate that some dog had his hands on what's mine."

"Yours?" My voice came out choked. "I'm not yours. I don't even know you. And I can fuck who I want."

"No, Love. You're mine. You just don't know it yet," he said. "And you're not going to fuck anyone else. You understand me?"

It was a command, and I found myself nodding without realizing it. Then I shook my head. "No. That's not how this works. You're a vampire. I belong to the shifters. You coming around here is going to get me killed. Do you understand that?"

"Is that all you're worried about?" He chuckled.

"Is that all?" My jaw dropped open. "What is wrong with you? I don't care how good you are in bed. No cock is worth death."

He groaned. "The way you say that word..."

I rolled my eyes. "This is over. You can't enter my apartment and I am done with this conversation." I started closing the door, keeping my eyes on him.

He watched me, as if daring me to open the door and invite him in. For a moment, I considered it, but regained my senses. Something about him made me feel so reckless. Like I wanted to be bad. It was dangerous. He was dangerous.

"See you soon, Love," he said.

I closed the door, then leaned against it, panting. *Fuck.* I was soaked. Good thing he couldn't get into my apartment. I wasn't sure my willpower would have held up. This vampire was going to get me into so much trouble.

# CHAPTER
# SIXTEEN

Isla

MORE DEAD VAMPIRES meant Ryder was blissfully too busy to come by my office. I'd never seen the pack so on edge. We were all pulled away from our usual business for a visit by the Supernatural Council. Which meant I spent the rest of the week securing catering orders and preparing the rarely used conference room.

Normally, I'd complain about being pulled away from my work, but Henry didn't have an assistant, and the rest of the pack was slammed. The shifters were rarely in the house because they were on patrol round the clock.

Considering that there was a serial killer on the loose, I was fine with having to do tasks I normally hated. Sure, I'd have twice as much work to catch up on tomorrow, but it gave me a break from worrying about how I'd react to Ryder.

Even the vampires sent to watch us were gone. There was a constant sense of dread, everyone wondering where they'd find the next body.

By Friday morning, the quiet I'd enjoyed all week was gone, replaced by the last minute frenzy of preparing for the Council.

Just as I finished setting out the plastic cups next to the water pitchers in the kitchen, Henry walked in with Ryder and Killian at his side. Ashley, Killian's daughter, was with them. I wasn't used to seeing other females around, but maybe they were hoping she'd help distract the Council. She was stunning and so far, no male had managed to tame her. In a lot of ways, I respected her for her high standards and focus on her own pleasure. Though I'd always suspected it was all a waiting game to get to Ryder.

"We're ready?" Henry asked.

I nodded, trying not to let my exasperation show. "Yes, boss. We're good. I got all the bases covered."

He frowned. "I don't want any of them sniffing around and finding anything they shouldn't."

"Dad, they're not here for us. We haven't done anything wrong. Unless you're the one draining vampires?" Ryder said.

"Of course not," Henry said. "But you can never drop your guard around the Council. They've destroyed whole families on a whim."

I winced, recalling the time they'd exiled an entire witch coven based on flimsy rumors that they were practicing illegal magic.

The Council was the governing body of Lost Harbor. Everything went through them and their authority was absolute. The Council was supposed to represent the whole town. Two shifters, two witches, two vampires, and two fae held titles on the council. There were even two empty places reserved for angels and demons if they ever returned. But no humans. No non-magical people. Just the supernaturals. It was another reason I needed out of this town. Humans had no protection.

"They're here," Killian said.

Henry's upper lip curled in disgust, then he took a deep breath and fixed his face into an impassive expression. "Let's get this over with."

I followed him and Ryder fell into step next to me. Goosebumps spread down my arms as I recalled our time in my office at the beginning of the week. This was the first time I'd seen him since then.

He glanced over at me and looked as if he might want to say something, but he returned his attention ahead of him without a word.

I left the alpha, Killian, and Ryder at the front door and headed to the conference room ahead of them. They'd greet all the guests and lead them to the meeting room. I was to stand in the corner and take notes. Like an assistant. I sighed, hating the role I had to play today.

Henry had said I'd look less threatening to the Council.

He and Killian were the only non-members permitted today, and adding another shifter might look like he was trying to hide something or some bullshit. Whatever the reason, I didn't press because I was curious. I'd never been permitted in any closed door meeting and it would be interesting to see what went on, even if I had to take notes during.

"Wait up," Ashley called.

I spun around, surprised to see her following me.

She stopped, then leaned in close, not hiding that she was smelling me.

I tensed, and my nose wrinkled. "What are you doing?"

"His scent is still on you. Weaker today, but it's still there," she said.

My heart pounded against my ribs, and my eyes widened. How did she know? If she could smell him...

"Are you and Ryder back together?" She crossed her arms over her chest.

I nearly laughed as the tension unwound. My mind went right to Dante, not Ryder. Something was very wrong with me.

"What's so funny?" Her eyes narrowed.

"Nothing. It's just that, never mind. We aren't a couple," I assured her.

"Then why have you smelled like him all week?" she demanded.

"I wasn't aware that you were smelling me." My brow furrowed. "I haven't even seen you this week."

"I have my ways," she said.

I felt violated. Who had been sniffing me when I didn't realize it? I really, really needed to get away from these shifters.

"Look, you need to let someone else have a chance. You've had your claws in him for too long. You're not even a wolf. You can't handle him," she said.

"And you can?" I shouldn't have said it. Why did I care if she and Ryder hooked up? Honestly, it would help me. Get him off my back. They should go for it. Get married, have babies, run this pack together. But her tone and her possessive nature instantly put me on guard.

"You know you don't belong here," she said.

"Look, we're not a couple. If he's not chasing after you, that's not my fault," I said.

She slapped me hard across the face. My hand went to the spot she'd hit, pressing into the sting. My eyes watered. "What the fuck, Ashley?"

"I've been nice to you because you were important to him. But he's done waiting for you. The whole pack knows you're fair game. This is the only warning I'm going to give you. Keep your hands off my man," she hissed.

"Does he know he's yours?" I asked, then dodged the fist she sent flying in my direction.

"What the fuck is going on here?" Ryder's voice made Ashley's next strike freeze midair.

She dropped her hand. "Nothing," she said, her tone sickly sweet.

I stifled a laugh and dropped my hand from my cheek.

If she was trying to get on his good side, she'd just made a huge mistake.

I didn't want Ryder to be hung up on me, but he was. And he was protective. Even if he said he was done. The last thing I wanted was to cause more drama. "We're fine," I assured him. "Just some girl talk."

I didn't need him to swoop in like some kind of knight in shining armor. Things were already complicated enough between us after sex in my office.

He narrowed his eyes. "You alright?"

I walked past Ashley without looking back at her. I could practically feel her eyes on me like daggers as I looped my arm through Ryder's. I shouldn't have. But maybe I had a death wish. Who knows?

"You know, I think Ashley's a little bit obsessed with you," I said, loud enough that I knew she could hear.

Ryder laughed. "Yeah, everyone knows that."

"We aren't a couple anymore," I reminded him. "You could be with her."

"I know," he said.

Our relationship had been good. The leaving me tied up in the coat check room was so completely out of character, it was easy to forget how scary it had been in the moment. Sometimes things felt simple with him, and I felt like I was settling back into old habits. But that was dangerous. I couldn't do that. I pulled my arm from his.

"You should be with someone who is going to make you happy." I wasn't sure that was Ashley, but I did want him to be happy. Maybe he and Ashley were perfect for each other. Maybe he'd kept that darker shifter side hidden because of my human frailty. He wouldn't have to hold back with someone like her.

He leaned in close and whispered in my ear, "Sex with you has ruined me for anyone else."

I shivered. "That's not fair, Ryder."

He shrugged. "It's true."

"I'm not that good," I said. "You must be with the wrong women."

"I've tried them all." He shrugged.

I shook my head, a smile on my face. "Of course you have." There really were no hard feelings. No jealousy, no regret. I enjoyed sex with him, but it didn't bother me that he wanted other women. I didn't want to be one of his harem, but I didn't need him to myself.

I realized I'd never told him that. "Ryder, you deserve to be with someone who will fight for you. And that's never going to be me."

Our conversation was cut short as footsteps and quiet conversation approached. Ryder went rigid, and the two of us moved to either side of the conference room doors.

Henry and Killian approached, followed by a group that I knew had to be the Supernatural Council. I'd never seen them in real life before, so I was surprised to note that half of them were much younger than I expected. Though, who knew what their real age was. Supernaturals didn't age the same way as humans.

The Council members filed into the room, none of them acknowledging me as they entered. After they were seated, I stepped inside, and Ryder closed the doors behind us.

He took the open seat at the table between his father and Killian. I stood in the corner where I'd stashed a notebook on a waiting chair. I knew my job today. Seen and not heard. Preferably melting into the background, so I wasn't even seen.

Sitting in the corner while a group of the most powerful supernaturals in all of Lost Harbor discussed a serial killer made me remember just how vulnerable and weak I was compared to the rest of them.

It was another reminder that the sooner I could get out of here, the better.

"How many have you found?" An older male with pointed ears and a long, lean physique asked.

I didn't need shifter senses to know he was fae. The way he carried himself and literally held his nose in the air told me everything. He hadn't waited for everyone to finish settling into the chairs and they hadn't made introductions. I supposed they all knew each other, so maybe it wasn't necessary.

Henry cleared his throat. "Always nice to see you, Alystor."

"Tell me why your son is here?" Alystor asked. "I thought we decided Council and you and your beta."

"I'm retiring soon, as you all know. Ryder should be part of this in case there are long term repercussions," Henry said.

"It's fine, Alystor," a younger looking female said. She

had the same lean build and pointed ears. Her hair was a brilliant blue that matched her eyes. Even her skin was tinted a pale blue. I wasn't sure what kind of fae she was, but I knew she had to be as lethal as she was beautiful.

"We're all concerned about this," a younger male with sandy blonde hair said. "We've got our people doing everything they can to see if they can find anything."

"While it's nice to hear your witches are sitting in prayer circles or something, us vampires are literally being bled alive. Nobody is coming to kill you, Gavin," the pale woman sitting next to Henry said.

"I'm going to be honest," Henry said. "We don't have any leads. I don't know why it's in our territory, and I don't know who might be responsible."

My brow furrowed, recalling the dead vampire at Marcus's place. There'd been wolf shifter blood on the silver used to bind him. I wasn't sure if they'd found that at the other sites, but it seemed like a lead to me.

I kept my mouth shut, though, and made a note that said, *no leads*. It felt stupid to write that down. I honestly wasn't even sure why I was here.

It was clear from the way this meeting started that nothing was going to be solved.

"How many?" Alystor repeated.

"Seventeen," Henry said.

My eyes widened. Seventeen dead vampires? That was far more than I'd heard about and I wouldn't put it past Henry to cover up a few if possible.

I added the information to my notes, then turned back

to the group. They were quiet for a moment, as if taking in the number.

"None of the dead vampires have any connection," the pale female vampire said. "We can't figure out why they go missing. They're all from different covens. They have different backgrounds, ages, and families. They don't even get their blood from the same donors."

"There has to be something," Alystor said. "You need to look deeper."

"We are. We have," the vampire said. "Perhaps you'd like to visit our territory and see what you can find?"

Alystor straightened. "I would be happy to assist."

Well, that actually sounded like progress. I made a note of it, but before I looked up from the paper, I felt the shift in the room.

It was as if the air had suddenly been sucked out. The silence that fell wasn't the same as the last one. A shiver ran down my spine.

"My invitation must have been misplaced," the words were like ice. Smooth and cold, with an edge of authority that made my skin tingle. I didn't have to look up to know who had just entered the room.

"Seventeen dead vampires and not a single lead?" Dante said.

The vampires rose from their places at the table and dropped into low bows. "Your highness."

The rest of the Council looked uneasy. I watched as Henry's hands balled into fists. Even the fae squirmed.

"How quickly manners are forgotten," he said. "This

Council serves in my stead. With me here, you have no authority unless I grant it to you."

"You've been gone for two hundred years and you want us to bow?" Gavin, the young witch, said. "We've been just fine without you."

Dante strolled over to the witch and stopped near his seat. Gavin's throat bobbed, but he maintained eye contact. My knuckles were white from how hard I was squeezing the pen in my hand.

Everyone was holding their breath, waiting to see what the king would do.

"You're young, so I'll give you a chance to repent for your disrespect," Dante said. "Especially since there are," he glanced at me, "females present."

Gavin scoffed. "You're a fossil from a time long ago. The world has changed in case you didn't notice while you were locked away in your coffin."

Dante set his palm on the sandy hair, his fingers tightening around the male's skull. Gavin reached for him, then his arms went slack and his jaw dropped.

"Let him go," the female witch said. "Stop. You're hurting him." She reached for Dante, but the vampire tossed her aside without releasing his grip on Gavin.

"Judging me when your sins are far worse," Dante said. Then, with both hands, he gripped the man's head and yanked.

With a tearing sound, Gavin's head separated from his body, his spine lifting from the hole where his neck had been attached. Blood spewed, and the body fell forward, landing with a thump on the conference table.

Screaming and cursing sounded, and I turned away, my stomach churning. I tried to hold back, but my breakfast was not going to stay put. Dropping the notebook, I raced for the trash can near the door and emptied the contents of my stomach.

A sickening thud made me jump, and I knew Dante had dropped the head. When I turned back, a pool of crimson was expanding across the table. The rest of the Council was on their feet, heads bowed.

Dante turned his gaze on me. I wondered if I should bow, but before I could make my body move, he looked away. "You may continue to serve this town. But you will better vet your members. If I find out any of you knew the activities that pathetic excuse for a male engaged in when nobody was looking, you'll join him in death."

"Wh-what activities?" The female witch managed, her face drained of color.

"You are very lucky you didn't know," Dante said.

I wasn't sure I wanted to know. Everyone in this town seemed to have a secret. Even I had my share. Well, I did now that Dante was in town. Before him, I'd been rather boring. Now, I had the fear of my pack finding out that I'd been with this monster. Twice.

Something was very, very wrong with me.

"When you are finished with your meeting, you will send a representative to my home to share what I missed. I want an update every day until the perpetrator is caught. Do you understand?" Dante said.

"I'll find someone," Henry said, quickly.

"I want her," Dante pointed to where I was still standing near the trash can.

"Oh, no, you don't want me," I said.

I saw the ghost of a smirk, but it was gone so quickly, I wasn't sure if I'd seen it.

"Isla's just a human. She's not involved in all this," Henry said.

"She's here, isn't she?" Dante asked.

"Just to take notes," Henry said.

"Then she sounds perfect," Dante said.

"I'm sure there's someone better suited," I said. "I have a lot of work around here."

Dante growled, but didn't look back at me. Still, the sound sent a trail of goosebumps down my arms.

"She'll do it," Henry said.

"Henry," I said, desperation in my tone.

"She'll do it and she won't complain," Henry hissed, giving me a hard glare.

I cursed under my breath. This was the last thing I needed. I was trying to get away from this deranged vampire who had some odd interest in me.

"Isla, please show me out so these fine folks can go back to their meeting." Dante whirled to me.

I looked over at Henry and Ryder, my expression pleading. This was the chance for Ryder to stand up for me, to do something to prove how desperately he wanted me.

Instead, he nodded encouragingly. His expression was similar to what you might give a child who was jumping into the pool without a life vest for the first time.

It made heat bubble and simmer inside. Something angry and bitter crawled beneath my skin. After all that he'd put me through, when it came down to it, he was nothing but talk.

Forcing my chin high, I walked to the door and pushed it open. "This way, *your highness.*" Snark dripped from each word, but he simply smiled and inclined his head before walking through the doors.

I'd give just about anything to hear what the Council had to say after the doors closed behind me, but I was busy escorting a murderer to the front door of the mansion.

The walk was silent, and thankfully, short. I opened the front door. "I imagine someone here knows your address for me to drop the notes off at?"

He stopped at the threshold, a wicked smile on his lips. "I'll send a car for you at five."

"I usually work late," I said.

"Six, then," he said.

The thought of being at his house after sunset made my stomach twist. He was ancient, so the sunlight didn't seem to bother him. But even the vampires in the Council room had come with umbrellas to prevent them from bursting into flames. Was he going to be surrounded by vampires the way Henry was always surrounded by wolf shifters?

"Why me?" I asked.

"You needed an excuse to be around me without getting yourself killed, right?"

"No," I nearly shouted. "I told you, I don't want anything to do with you."

"You still smell like a dog," he said. "We need to remedy that."

"That is never going to happen," I said. "It was a mistake."

"What's that expression? Fool me once, shame on me; fool me twice..."

"You should go," I said.

"My driver will be here at six." His silver eyes flicked down my body, moving slowly upward until he reached my eyes.

I sucked in a breath, biting down on the inside of my cheek to keep myself from falling into his seduction. Why was every move he made so sensual? Why was I finding it difficult to stay mad at him?

I had just watched him rip someone's spine from their body. He was not a good guy.

He'd warned me.

And I hadn't listened.

And I was struggling to listen to myself even now.

"I need to get back to work," I said. "Someone's going to have to clean up that mess you left behind."

"Some of my best work," he said. "See you later, Love."

Gratefully, I closed the door behind him. My heart hammered against my ribs and my whole body felt flush with heat. He was a monster. And something was very, very wrong with me because there was a little part of me that still wanted him.

# CHAPTER
# SEVENTEEN

Isla

THE REST of the meeting was a blur. Derek came into the room with a couple of other shifters and hauled the dead witch out. Someone shoved the head, spine still attached, into a large black garbage bag. Towels were used to wipe up the blood, and they casually sprayed cleaning solution on the table to remove the red tint. They moved as if this was something they did all the time.

I guess that was what he did for Henry.

Nobody batted an eye as they dragged out the body. I tried to focus on what was being said and scribbled nonsense words on my paper. The problem was, there wasn't much to say.

The Council agreed that they wanted the vampire king

gone, but to do that, they had to figure out who was killing the vampires.

Nobody had a lead.

"Do you want help on patrols in your territory?" The fae male asked the vampires.

"I'm not sure our people would take kindly to having outsiders watching us," she said.

"We're all in danger with the king here. What happened to Gavin could be any of us," Henry pointed out. "He's already got several of his blood suckers stationed at my home round the clock."

"He sent one to monitor us," the female vampire said. "And we are guessing there's a few more we don't know of who report to him. He doesn't even trust his own kind."

"We can't afford to keep finding these bodies," Henry said.

"We can't afford for it to stop before we catch the killer, either," the fae male said. "Not that I want more death, but if the killer gets wind of this and remains hidden, we run the risk of having a new king in town for a long while."

"I've heard the stories of what it was like under his rule," the female witch said. "I'm not immortal. I don't want to spend the rest of my life under that kind of terror."

My chest tightened. What was she talking about? We'd all grown up hearing how dangerous vampires were, but I always figured that was because I was in wolf shifter territory. Even now, the vampires didn't get along with us.

But what had things been like here when a vampire had ruled all the supernaturals?

"You're right," the male vampire said. "We need help. The killer is clearly taking our people from our territory and dropping them in yours. We could use increased eyes in both territories."

"I can send my people in if you'll assure me of their safety," the fae male said.

The male vampire nodded. "You have my word."

"We can contribute to the patrols in the shifter territory," the witch said. "And if you agree, I can send a team in to see if we can find any traces of magic in the places you discovered the bodies."

Henry nodded. "You have safe passage through our land."

"We are running out of time," the female vampire said. "The king can go months without feeding, but his blood-lust is legendary. Those he travels with are among the most ancient of our kind. Even if they intend to keep a meal alive, they require so much at each feeding that there can be... accidents."

"Should we send an offering?" The female fae asked. "Some humans to help take the edge off?"

"What?" I stood. "In case you forgot, humans have feelings, and families, and lives. We're not disposable."

"Isla, sit down," Henry hissed.

"No." I took a step closer to the table. "There are no human representatives on this Council, but we live here too. And unlike the rest of you, we're stuck here."

"She has a point," Ryder said.

I appreciated him finally saying something on my behalf, but it was too little too late. He'd done nothing while the king had demanded my presence at his home. Where maybe I'd become that next meal.

"Leave us out of this," I demanded. "This isn't our fight. You get enough from us as it is. The vampires already have their systems for feeding. If you want to drop off bagged blood, do it. But don't put my fellow humans at risk," I said.

"Our donors choose to give us blood from their veins," the female vampire said.

"Because the alternative is to join another supernatural group or die of starvation on the fringes of society," I said.

"Isla, that's enough," Henry's tone was harsh, but I didn't care.

"Nice to see that there's still fire left in some of the humans," the fae male said. His feline smirk was unsettling. "You are welcome to visit us any time you'd like, little one."

I glared at him. Of all the creatures at this table, the fae were the most dangerous. Possibly even more dangerous than the vampire king. I knew better than to accept or even thank him for the offer, so I simply nodded. I wasn't in the mood to play games with the fae today.

"We will send an offering of bagged blood," the female vampire said. "How does that sound?"

I nodded, surprised at how tense every muscle in my body felt. "That's good, thank you."

"Sit, Isla," Henry said. "Your humans are safe."

"We'll send some after this meeting. Maybe it'll take the edge off before you pay him a visit," the male vampire said. "I can't imagine how he'll react if you speak to him the way you just spoke to us."

I gritted my teeth and bit back the insult I wanted to shout at him. He was bating me, trying to get me to say something I'd regret. Stupid supernaturals.

I thought wolves were bad but now I was dealing with the others on a level I never expected. When you were a human living among the monsters, it was best to stay invisible.

I wasn't anymore.

They'd all be waiting to hear what happened after I visited the king.

"I think that's enough for today," Henry said. "Let's meet again in a week, unless something happens sooner."

As they said their goodbyes and filed out of the room, I shrunk to the back, waiting for them to clear before I left.

Henry hung back after the room cleared, then rounded on me. "You ever step out of line like that again, and I'll kill you myself."

"Maybe the king will beat you to it," I snapped.

"I hope he does. You've gotten too full of yourself over the years. I can find someone to replace you with a snap of my fingers. The only thing keeping you alive is that Ryder would mourn you and I need his head clear for this transition of power. But don't think that'll keep you safe. The more his wolf matures, the less he'll care about insignificant things like you. One of these days, he'll dispose of you himself and I will enjoy the hell out of watching that." He smiled, but it was cruel and cold and didn't reach his eyes.

I kept my mouth shut. I wanted to punch him in the face. Or kick him in the balls. Either way, I wanted to cause him just a little of the pain I'd felt growing up here.

But it wasn't worth it. I was free to come and go as I pleased, and I needed that freedom to make it to my escape.

As long as the vampire king let me live.

How had things gotten so complicated?

"When you visit him tonight, I need you to pay attention to everything. I want to know how many he's got in his inner circle. I want to know what he's planning. How long he intends to stay. And mostly, why he's really here," Henry said.

"You don't think he's here for the dead vampires?" I asked.

"You think someone like him gives a shit about a few dead vamps?" Henry shook his head. "All the dead vampires were newer. Most of them under a hundred years old. He doesn't even know them personally."

"Maybe he cares about his kind?" I asked.

Henry laughed. "Such a human thing to say. Vampires aren't like shifters. They don't have a pack. They might have a few they care about. Those would be the group he travels with. Other than that, he won't care."

"You think he's going to tell me these things?" I asked.

Henry charged forward, and I backed away until I was standing flush against the wall. He caged me in, his hands on either side of my head. "You are your mother's daughter. You have ways of getting men to talk. He might be ancient, and he might be a monster, but when it comes to his needs, they're the same as any man."

Henry grabbed my chin with his hand and lifted my face. "You get him to talk. You understand me?"

"Let go of me," I said.

He grinned, then dropped his hands. I moved to the side, trying to get away from him, but he pinned me with his body. His hips pressed against my waist and I gasped at the sudden feel of him against me. He grabbed my breasts and squeezed. "I own you."

I squirmed and grabbed at his arms. "You're a pig."

His hands moved to my face, cupping my cheeks. "I'm just waiting for the day when you come to me. Ryder is a boy. When you're ready for a man, you let me know."

He let go of me and stepped back.

I moved fast, creating space between us before he grabbed me again. Not bothering to go back for the abandoned notebook, I headed for the door.

"Remember, I want all the information. You work for me," Henry called after me.

# CHAPTER
# EIGHTEEN

Isla

I RECOGNIZED the driver as one of the vampires I'd seen stalking around the Crescent Pack house. Luke, I think.

He was silent as we drove to wherever Dante lived. I realized I hadn't even asked, not that it mattered. I'd never been in vampire territory before, but I didn't know if that was where he was staying. Had he moved into some abandoned house or joined another family? Or maybe they kept a dusty old mansion somewhere off the beaten path.

The car slowed, turning on a dirt road near the cemetery, then he turned into the cemetery itself on a practically overgrown dirt road I'd never noticed. The cemetery was large, and I knew it was the border between shifter and vampire territories, but I didn't think of using it as a way to get between them. Not that I'd ever spent time considering it. It would be suicidal for me to go to the vampire lands. Especially at night.

The headstones looked eerie in the headlights, but I'd much rather spend the night alone there than spend even an hour at Dante's place.

We were farther than I'd gone, and the graves seemed to stretch forever. I had no idea just how large the space was.

Finally, I caught sight of a building at what appeared to be the end of the cemetery. No, not a building, a fucking castle. "Seriously?" The word came out unbidden.

Luke laughed. "Right? A little on the nose, isn't it? Vampire in a crumbling old castle."

I smiled, despite myself. "I'm sure you can't tell him that."

"Dante? Oh, he hates this fucking place. Why do you think he's been gone so long? Nothing but bad memories," he said.

My brow furrowed. I thought I was going to have to pry information from the vampires to get anything that Henry might consider juicy enough to leave me alone.

I shuddered at the reminder of his touch. He'd never once touched me like that. Henry wasn't good, not by a long shot, but he had some standards. His companions were usually older than me and I'd never heard talk of him forcing himself on them. The fact that he thought I'd come to him willingly made bile rise in my throat.

"Why's he here, then?" I asked, desperate to clear that vision of Henry so close to me from my mind.

"Not my place to say," Luke said. "You can ask him yourself."

I frowned. So much for getting information easily.

We pulled up to a wrought iron gate, where two males were standing as guards. Luke rolled down the window and signaled. The doors opened, and the guards stepped aside.

The car inched forward, the wheels crunching over the long gravel driveway until we came to a halt in front of the castle. The building was like a cross between a medieval castle and a southern plantation. Huge gray stone columns lined the entry, but instead of supporting a porch, they held a pediment topped with gargoyles.

The structure rose two stories above the pediment. Windows with iron bars on the edges and a circular rose window in the center. Everything about the structure was off. Like someone had taken the bits and pieces they enjoyed from several different architectural periods and put them together into one building. None of it worked.

I shook my head at the ostentatious entry. It was over-whelming and over the top, but it had also clearly seen better days. Some of the stone creatures were missing their wings, and the giant rose window on the façade had chunks of glass missing.

The sun was dipping lower in the sky, but it was still enough daylight to keep many vampires indoors. Luke didn't seem to have any issue with the light, and I already knew that Dante didn't even flinch from the sun.

Hopefully, I could make this quick and be back home before the sky was fully dark.

Luke took the steps two at a time, reaching the huge wood door to pull it open before I reached it. My heart hammered against my ribs as I crossed the threshold.

The interior was in even more disrepair than the exterior. Dirty and worn rugs spanned the scuffed wood floors. Chandeliers covered in dust and spider webs swayed at the slightest breeze. A few buzzing lights mounted to the walls gave minimal illumination. The halls were lined with rickety tables topped with marble sculptures coated in thick dust. Yellowing paintings hung cooked on the peeling wallpaper.

Nobody had bothered to care for this place. It was obvious that Dante didn't care about this house. Which made the question even more intense. Why was he here?

I couldn't shake what Henry had said. How would he have even heard about dead vampires in our little slice of the world, let alone care enough to come all the way here? He'd been away for so long. Why now?

"Isla, right on time," Dante's silken voice shivered down my spine like a caress.

I spun to see him walking down the stairs. "Are you sure that's safe?"

His brow furrowed.

I inclined my head toward the steps. "From the looks of the place, your foot might go right through the boards."

He chuckled. "It's happened before. Come, there is a space that was built in the last century."

"While you were away?" It was odd that something had been done while the rest of the house had been left to rot.

"I had a feeling I'd end up back here, eventually. Though, I had hoped it would be to add a body to the family plot."

"Hoped?" I lifted a brow.

"When you've lived as long as I have, death is no longer a burden, but rather, a release," he said.

"Does that mean you figured you'd be dead next time you came here?" I asked as I followed in step behind him.

"Perhaps." He led me to a kitchen that was more dungeon than cooking space. It was windowless, and the stove looked like it belonged in a museum. There was no refrigerator or microwave and the only sign that anyone used the space was the stovetop espresso pot.

A spindly table with another thick layer of dust was surrounded by a few wobbly looking chairs. For a house this grand, nothing inside it appeared to be super high end. It was basic, simple furniture. The faded and neglected art in the entry the only hint at what might have once been a luxurious estate.

At the end of the kitchen was a battered screen door. When I stepped through, I understood why he'd brought me here.

We were indeed in the newest looking room I'd seen so far, even if it still gave off the feelings of visiting an elderly female.

The screened-in porch was carefully decorated with wicker furniture in bright white topped with colorful pillows. A sleek glass table sat between the chairs and fairy lights hung on the walls, giving the place a whimsical glow.

"This is not what I expected," I said.

"Would you rather I take you to the tomb I'm guessing you think I sleep in?" he asked.

My throat suddenly went dry at the thought of seeing where he slept, and it had nothing to do with it being a tomb. Something was so very wrong with me.

He turned to face me. "Or the throne room where the pathetic sycophants who came to pledge their loyalty wait for me?"

"No, this is good. Better," I said.

He sat on a wicker love seat and patted his hand on the space next to him. "Sit."

I narrowed my eyes. "I'm not a dog."

"You still smell like one," he said.

"What I smell like is none of your concern," I said.

"It very much is my concern. I don't enjoy sharing my toys," he said.

"I am not your toy," I hissed.

He smirked. "Why can I smell your arousal?"

I gritted my teeth. Stupid supernaturals. "You are a mistaken."

"Sit." He inclined his head. "Please."

"Let's get this over with." I took a single chair across the table from him. There was no way I would risk sitting so close to him. For one, he was fucking dangerous. And two, I didn't trust myself around him.

"Why am I here?" I asked.

"You told me they'd kill you if they knew you were with me. Now, you don't have a choice. They'll all know and they can't harm you for it," he said.

"So in your head, you figured you'd force me to come over here and I'd just beg for your cock?" I glared at him defiantly.

He groaned. "I love the way you say that word. You have a beautifully filthy mouth. I can't wait until I see it wrapped around my dick."

"It's not going to happen," I said. "This is not a booty call."

"Booty call. I hate that term. It always makes me think of frat boys and unsatisfied partners." He leaned forward, his elbows resting on his knees. "I promise you, my partners are always satisfied."

"Well, that's nice. Find someone else," I said. "Fucking you isn't worth the risk to my life."

"They'll smell me on you no matter what now," he said. "Besides, I could simply tell them what happened at the party."

"You're an asshole," I said.

"Based on your dating history, I think you might be into assholes," he said.

"This conversation is over. Get to the point. I have things to do that aren't you," I snapped.

I should probably watch what I say. This male could

kill me before I even opened my mouth to scream, but he was having more fun flirting with me.

So much ego. He could likely have his choice of female, but he seemed to be fixated on me. Maybe he wanted to see how far he could push it before the Crescent Pack did end my life. He was probably the type that got off on violence.

"Fine. You want to get right to business?" he asked.

I lifted my brows, waiting for him to get it over with.

"I need information on the Crescent Pack. And you're going to get it for me," he said.

"Funny, that's the same thing Henry asked me to do with you," I said.

"I figured. Tell him whatever you want. I've got nothing to hide." He stretched his arms across the top of the love seat and his legs spread wide. His huge frame took up most of the couch.

I swallowed hard and for a moment, I recalled the fact that his large size related to everything about him. His cock would most definitely choke me if I went down on him.

Clearing my throat, I shook the thought away. What the fuck was wrong with me?

He smirked. "I get the sense that you have things you'd like to hide."

"Nope." My voice was too high pitched. "Just your normal human stuck in the vicious cycle that is life in Lost Harbor."

"What did your alpha want to know about me?" he asked.

"He's not my alpha," I said.

"Okay. What did he want?" Dante asked.

"He wanted to know about you," I said.

"That's sweet, but I'm not into shifters on a power trip," he said.

I fought against the smile. "Cute."

"Most women think so," he said.

"I'm sure they do, but I'm not most women," I said.

"Oh, I know," he said.

I stood. "Well, we're getting nowhere."

"Sit back down." His voice had an edge, a level of authority that made the hair on the back of my neck stand on edge.

My eyes widened. Something in that tone seemed to call to a primal part of me. To my surprise, I sat.

"Good girl," he said. "Now, let's discuss what you're going to do for me."

"I don't want to spy on the pack. Leave me out of this," I said.

"You're going to spy on them for me because if you don't, I'm going to share about our time together." He leaned forward again. The humor in his expression was gone, replaced by something hard and cold. His silver eyes were like ice.

"You said they'd kill you if they knew," he reminded me. "Is that true?"

I nodded.

"Then I guess you work for me," he said with a grin.

I balled my hands into fists. "They don't know who's killing the vampires."

"I don't give a shit about dead vampires," he said. "I'm looking for someone more dangerous. Someone I think your alpha might be helping."

"If you think he tells me things, you're deluded," I said. "I cook the books. That's it."

"Which makes you the most powerful person in his organization," he said.

"If it weren't me, he'd just find someone else," I said.

Dante shook his head. "No. He wouldn't have you doing this for so long if he thought he could get a shifter in there instead."

I frowned. It was probably true. "Listen, you want the dirt on his illegal enterprises? That I can do. But I don't get names or information. I fix illegal things to make them look legit."

"How long has the pack been pushing lotus?" Dante asked.

My chest tightened. Nobody talked about the drug that had been sweeping through the human residents. It was toxic even in small doses to supernaturals and lethal to vampires. It was a newer drug, still only discussed in whispers. I'd only seen it in real life once.

I shook my head. "No way they're involved with that. Supernaturals don't want to touch the stuff."

"I'm sure there's a few who dabble," he said.

"It's lethal," I said.

"For vampires, yes, but for everyone else, it's about balance," he said.

I scowled. "I didn't take you as the drug lord type, but if you're here to push out the competition, I don't think you're looking in the right place."

He rose to his feet in a powerful, predatory movement. His face darkened with anger. "Do not confuse me for a low life drug dealer."

I flinched, but quickly forced myself to bite back the fear rising like dark tendrils, threatening to pull me under. "Don't you dare come at me like that and try to sell yourself as some kind of hero. I watched you kill that witch today. You're no hero."

His eyes narrowed. "I never said I was."

I stood, lifting my chin so I was looking into his eyes. "Find yourself another patsy. I'm not doing it."

Dante's hand moved to the back of my head, his fingers tangling into my hair. He yanked me forward, and I grunted as I tried to resist. He was too strong, easily pulling me closer.

I continued to stare at him, my breaths coming out in pants. His nostrils flared and his liquid silver eyes were hungry and dangerous.

Goosebumps erupted across my skin, and tension coiled low in my belly.

He grabbed my chin with his free hand. "You will find out the information I need because if your pack doesn't kill you for your disobedience, I will."

My skin felt hot at the points of contact and I couldn't

remember the last time I felt so alive.

When he released me and stepped away, I nearly whimpered at the empty feeling remaining. Thankfully, I managed to keep myself contained.

He was a murderer, a monster. Just like everyone else in this town. The wetness in my panties was proof I needed out of here. Growing up in this place had broken me. Made me desire things I shouldn't. I knew it was wrong. I also knew if he'd kissed me, I would have kissed him back. Even though he'd just threatened my life.

I was all sorts of fucked up.

"Now, be a good girl and find out how your pack is involved in the lotus trade. I need to know everything, no matter how insignificant it might seem," he said.

The lust cleared, making me think properly again. "I hate you."

"I know, Love," he said. "Go on. I'll expect information by the end of the week."

In my dreams that night, Dante's hand went around my throat, tightening until I gasped for air. His hands kneaded my breasts, his tongue swirled around my clit, and he expertly thrust his cock inside me until I came so hard I saw stars. I woke with soaked panties and hair stuck to the sweat on my face.

The worst part was that I had to get myself off after the dream just to help myself fall back asleep. And when I did, I pictured Dante doing all sorts of terrible things to me.

There really is something very wrong with me.

# CHAPTER
## NINETEEN

Isla

DANTE'S THREATS and instructions were like a heavy weight in my gut, making everything so much harder than it should be. I questioned each receipt, each transaction, every invoice.

After digging through the piles on my desk, I didn't even find a sign of anything illegal, let alone anything linking to the mysterious new drug.

Lotus wasn't a topic that was brought up often. It had appeared in Lost Harbor sometime in the last year, and nobody knew where it came from. Humans were the only users as far as I knew, and while the shifters didn't like it, they didn't actively try to stop it. At least, not that I was aware of.

The more I thought about it, the more it made sense

that the Crescent Pack would be involved. If it was something that kept humans loyal and got them to part with their limited funds, the Crescent Pack would jump at the opportunity.

I knew most of the illegal activities that went on. Money laundering, arms deals, lots of trading in black magic and illegal herbs. The Crescent Pack didn't even deal traditional drugs. That was more fae territory.

My office door swung open, and I looked up from my computer. Henry's huge frame filled up the door and he crossed the room before dropping into the chair in front of my desk.

"Good morning to you too, boss," I said.

"You didn't come see me this morning," he said. "I thought you were dead."

"You seem real broken up about it," I said.

He grunted. "You went to see him?"

*Dante.* I went to see Dante. "Yeah, I did."

Henry lifted his hands in the air. "And?"

"He's investigating the dead vampires." I wasn't sure why I lied. I knew nothing about the broody vampire king, but I was starting to think I might not know as much about the Crescent Pack as I thought, either.

The only thing I did know was that between Henry and Dante, I was pretty sure Dante was the more dangerous. Staying on his good side until one of us left town felt like it was better odds for survival.

Henry lifted a surprised brow. "Really?"

I shrugged. "Seems that way, boss. He was pretty closed off around me. I'm sure he doesn't trust me."

He grunted again. "He's lying."

"Probably," I agreed. "Everyone knows you can't trust a vampire."

"That's the damn truth," he said. "Who was with him?"

"Nobody," I said. "He had someone pick me up and take me there, but I didn't see anyone else. I think he took me to a different part of the house, away from the other vampires."

"Interesting. He's hiding you. Or he thinks they'll eat you," he said, tapping a finger on his chin.

I turned my attention back to my work, hoping that would let Henry know I was done with the conversation.

"You're going to see him again, right?" Henry asked.

I looked up, surprised by how much my heart kicked in my chest at the thought. "I suppose."

"Good. I need you to get more out of him. Remember what we talked about," he said.

"How could I forget?" I asked.

"Make him trust you," Henry said. "Find out the truth."

"Got it," I said, already set on telling Henry nothing. I'd forgotten about Henry's insistence that I whore myself out for information. I no longer felt any guilt for lying to my boss.

The laws were clear. If I cozied up to a vampire, my life was forfeit. Yet, that was what he was asking me to do.

There was zero guarantee he wouldn't use that against me to silence me. Especially if he was doing shady things that even I didn't know about.

A gentle knock sounded on my open door. "Sorry to interrupt, boss." Derek stood at the door. "You told me you wanted to know right away."

Henry bristled, instantly turning his attention from me. "You found Marcus?"

Derek glanced at me, then back at Henry.

"Well? Fucking spit it out," Henry demanded.

One more glance at me. I didn't move. I didn't breathe. Whatever this was, Derek didn't want to share in front of me.

Henry let out a low growl.

"We found Marcus. Well, what's left of him," Derek said.

"If you're telling me this, it means you're not doing what I pay you to do," Henry said.

My whole body tensed. Marcus. Of course. How had I forgotten that? Marcus paid more money for protection than any of the other accounts. If someone was involved with lotus, they'd be making bank, and they'd be pissing off all the supernaturals.

One of the only things the various species had in common was their disdain for the drug. It was dangerous. For once, there was something that humans were impervious to that could kill them. If the humans started slipping it into food...

What if Marcus was the one dealing the lotus? What if someone tried to put an end to his business?

"You need to see the body," Derek said. "Well, what's left of it, that is."

I squirmed just enough in my chair at that comment that both shifters turned to look at me.

Henry grinned. "Take Isla with you. She'll report back what she sees."

"That's not my job, Henry," I snapped. "I math. I number. I don't evaluate dead bodies."

"You're whatever I say you are," he said. "Get Gina up here. She'll take over the books. Until this vampire king is gone, your job is finding out everything you can about him."

"I don't see how looking at a mangled body helps," I said, my stomach already churning.

"After she sees it, drop her at his place. Let her tell him the update. A peace offering, from us, to the king," Henry said.

I wasn't in a hurry to see Dante again so soon. "He told me to come back at the end of the week."

"He told me to let him know if I heard anything. Marcus was our primary suspect. If he's dead, the king should know," Henry said.

My brow furrowed. Marcus's name hadn't been brought up in the Council meeting. While I agree it looked suspicious that there was a dead vampire in his garage and he was missing, I hadn't heard his name since that day we found the body.

"You sure you want her to see this, boss? It's pretty gruesome," Derek said. "And that's coming from me."

More secrets. More things about the pack I didn't know. I knew Derek was high ranking and that he did questionable things, but if it was so much worse than the stuff I did know about, I wasn't sure I wanted to be alone with him.

"Just go. Show her and take care of the mess," Henry said. "Make sure she has something good to tell the vampire."

I didn't want to go, but I knew that my objections wouldn't be any stronger than Derek. "Should we bring someone else along?"

"No. Nobody else involved, you understand? Not even Ryder," Henry said.

My insides twisted uncomfortably. What the fuck was I getting involved with?

"Let's go," Derek said.

The first several minutes of the ride were quiet. I gripped the armrest on the door and my whole body was tense and small. I didn't like being alone with Derek. The air in the car felt stale and suffocating and I just hoped that wherever we were going wasn't much farther.

"Is that why you broke up with Ryder? Decided to trade in the son for the father?" Derek asked.

"Of course not. You really think he'd be sending me off to do something like this if he was concerned about my well-being?" I asked.

"You don't have to be concerned about someone to fuck them," Derek said matter-of-factly.

Well, he had a point. Hadn't I gone right for the pleasure over the emotions when I had taken the king into the closet? My jaw tightened as regret swirled.

Go figure the one time I choose to be reckless and it ends up costing far more than I'd been willing to give. I had to believe I wouldn't be in this mess right now if I hadn't given in to my desires. The king would be demanding some other random girl be meeting with him for the dirt on the shifters. Or maybe not. He needed someone on the inside and being human, I probably seemed the weakest link.

"I get why you broke up with him. You're smart, and I don't think a boy like Ryder can give you what you want." He reached over and set his hand on my knee. "You need a man. Someone like me."

I had to resist the urge to roll my eyes into the back of my head at the presumptuous and cheesy line. As if touching something foul, I gently lifted his hand off my knee and set it on his. "I'm not in the market for any companionship right now, but thank you for the offer."

I wanted to tell him how inappropriate his flirting was and how the two of us together was never going to happen. But I had a strong enough sense of self-preservation to know not to cross someone like him. I never realized just how terrible all the males in the pack were. I suppose Ryder had protected me in his own way. None of them so much as flirted with me while we were together. I could handle the jealous girls, but these vile old men were something I had not prepared for.

Derek shrugged. "You know where to find me if you change your mind."

I forced a strained smile on my face and nodded, hoping this was the end of this topic. Desperate to discuss anything else, I thought about what we were actually doing. We weren't on a date or going anywhere interesting. This was business, and I was in for something gruesome. "Any sage advice on what I can do to prepare myself for what I'm about to see?"

"When did you last eat?" Derek glanced at me, then returned his eyes to the road.

"Couple hours ago," I said. "But I'm not hungry."

"I wasn't asking so we could stop for food. I'm curious how much vomit I should expect," he said.

"How bad is it? I saw the vampire at Marcus's place and kept my lunch down there," I said. He didn't need to know that the cracking and broken bones administered by Dante had pushed me over the edge. Normally, I had a steel stomach. But that day had pushed me to my breaking point. And again when Dante ripped out the witch's spine. So maybe I was a vomit risk.

"I really don't want to talk about it," Derek said. "A few of my guys are there, ready to collect all the pieces and eliminate the evidence. I've done a lot of this for Henry over the years, but this is the worst one I've ever seen."

"I never actually knew what you did for him. There's that many bodies to dispose of?" I asked.

"There's always something or someone to dispose of. Even you have to have figured that out by now. You see everything, the numbers don't lie. I imagine the only reason you stay in the dark about some parts is because you simply don't want to know," he said.

My chest tightened as I recalled what Dante had said. He seemed to think the same thing. That I knew everything that went on in the Crescent Pack, but I didn't. I saw receipts and invoices. I got notes about what to charge and who to pay. It wasn't like they wrote down the exact thing that each of these shifters did. "I think you misunderstand what my job is."

"I think you don't like to wonder about the checks you write or the deposits you make," he said.

"That's all I do. Henry tells me to pay someone and I pay them. He even tells me what type of service to write it up as. How would I know anything else?" He had a point about the fact that I didn't want to know. When I first started this, I'll admit I was curious. But back then, I was new to being involved in the pack on such an intimate level. The more things I found out, the more I wished I didn't know.

"You knew enough to be polite when you declined my advance." Derek grinned. "I appreciate that you let me down gently, but I know it's because you're afraid of me. You know more than you realize."

"What did Marcus do? I don't even know that. He paid more than any other shifter for protection from our pack, but I never knew what he did."

"Marcus was a scumbag. He had his fingers in everything, but if he hadn't paid us protection, he would have moved to a different territory and paid someone else. So Henry let him get away with everything. I'll tell you this much, Lost Harbor is a better place now that he's dead," Derek said.

A chill ran down my spine. "You're just proving my point. All of that was secret. Hidden."

"Was it?" Derek pulled the car off the side of the road near an open wooded space that existed as a buffer between our territory and the witch territory. "Who hated Marcus more than anyone?"

Henry seemed to barely tolerate him, and for most people, Marcus was a necessary evil if you needed your car fixed. I couldn't think of anyone who actually liked the man. I couldn't think of a single person who would call him a friend.

Then I remembered how pissed Jimmy had been about having to go check on the man. My brow furrowed as I considered what I knew about him. Jimmy was another monster. Someone who earned their reputation and could likely never fully wash off the blood that stained his hands. But part of that reputation came from what he did when he found out what had happened to his sister.

My heart ricocheted against my ribs and I realized that I did know what Marcus was involved in. There were black markets for everything here. Including people. Or in the case of Jimmy's sister, shifters. It was one of the few things humans didn't have to worry about. Since we couldn't go

169

through the barrier, no one could steal us and take us away. But Jimmy's sister wasn't so lucky.

She was a full wolf shifter from a long line of pure wolf shifters. Making her especially valuable to those crazy people who thought bloodlines mattered more than anything else. I knew she'd been taken, sold somewhere outside of Lost Harbor. Jimmy had brutally killed everyone who was involved, but he'd been too late. If his sister was still alive, she was somewhere far away.

My heart softened a bit for the grumpy shifter. I suddenly felt I'd been too harsh on the way I viewed him. He was dangerous, but I suddenly realized I'd take his kind of dangerous over any of the others.

"Does Jimmy know? What Marcus did?" I asked carefully.

"So you figured it out. I told you that you know more than you realize. And no, if Jimmy knew Marcus was involved, he would have been dead fifteen years ago," Derek said.

"I hope it was painful." My words startled me; I'd never seen myself as the type who hoped for vengeance. But someone like Marcus deserved the worst possible death.

"Come see for yourself." Derek opened the car door and stepped out. I followed.

# CHAPTER
# TWENTY

Isla

NOTHING COULD HAVE PREPARED me for what I walked into.

My stomach churned, but the dark part of me that was glad he was dead kept the bile from rising. If anyone deserved this, it was Marcus.

He wasn't just dead. He'd been torn to pieces.

Limbs hung from trees, entrails stretched across the dirt. His head lay under a tree, the eyes picked out by birds, the skin gnawed and peeled away.

He hadn't been here long enough for the earth to claim his body, just long enough for the creatures who lived here to munch on him.

"What's she doing here?" Jack, a lanky shifter with bleached blonde hair, asked.

"Henry wanted her to be able to report what she saw to that king dude," Derek said.

I tore my gaze from the scattered body parts and looked around at the gathered males. I recognized all of them. Aside from Jack, Amir and Pete were waiting under the trees. All of them were wearing gloves. Amir had a pair of goggles hanging from his neck, and Pete was holding a few black trash bags.

"You ever seen anything like this before?" I asked nobody in particular.

"Not quite like this," Derek said. "We've seen limbs torn off."

"Who hasn't?" Jack added.

Even I'd seen that. "Why *in* the trees?" It was like a gruesome decoration.

"I have no idea," Derek said. "That's why I told Henry to come see. Even if they were thrown, that would take a few tries."

I shuddered. "Gross."

"Yeah," Jack agreed.

"What are you going to do with him?" I asked.

"We'll take care of it, and nobody will know," Derek said.

"Boss wants it gone completely?" Amir sounded surprised. "He doesn't still think he's the one..."

"You can talk in front of her," Derek said. "Henry did."

Amir nodded, but looked uncomfortable. "I mean, if he's the vamp killer, who took him out?"

The realization hit hard, and I blew out a breath. "That

must be what Henry's after. He wants me to find out if the king did this."

"I gotta admit, whoever did this was powerful. That ancient fucker would explain a lot," Derek said.

"I'll see what I can find out." Maybe I'd get lucky. Maybe Marcus really was the killer and this could all be over with. But then there was still the lotus the king had asked me about. He'd made it clear he didn't give a shit about the dead vampires.

"You don't think Marcus was involved in other things," I started, keeping my tone almost bored, "Like lotus, for example?"

All the shifters tensed. Amir, Pete, and Jack all turned to Derek. I followed their lead and turned my attention to the older shifter. He lifted his brows. "You looking for a fix, little one?"

"Not at all," I said. "I just wondered if he was part of that problem."

"I don't think so, but it's possible. That's a better question for a human," he said.

"Yeah, good point," I said, hoping I hadn't drawn suspicion with my question.

"Go ahead and make this go away. I'm going to run Isla to the vamp's house," Derek said.

There was no conversation on this drive and I was afraid to bring anything up. I would rather Derek forget I'd ever asked about lotus. Internally, I was cursing myself for even asking. I didn't need to actually put effort into helping Dante. If he wanted to hurt me, he'd likely do it either way.

"You need me to stay?" Derek asked as he parked in front of the crumbling mansion.

"I'll be fine," I said. Worst case, I could walk home through the cemetery. It wasn't all that far.

"Good luck," he said.

The front door opened before I could even knock. Dante smiled at me. "To what do I owe this pleasure?"

His fangs were on full display and there was a spot of blood on the side of his lips. I glanced behind me, suddenly wishing I'd asked Derek to stay. The car was already down the driveway, a cloud of dust in its wake.

I turned back to Dante. "You have something or someone," I touched the side of my lip, "right here."

His tongue darted out and licked the blood off. A shiver ran through me and my mind went straight to recalling what that tongue could do. "You caught me during lunch."

I should be afraid of him. The blood was a reminder of what he was and what he was capable of. But I couldn't bring myself to fear him. I was cautious, sure, but not afraid. I was broken.

"Henry sent me," I said. "To give you an update."

"Well, why don't you come in?" He swept his arm toward the interior of the house.

I hesitated, then sucked in a breath and followed him.

A leggy blonde woman was sprawled out on the floral

couch in the front room. I could see the bright scarlet blood on her neck; remnants of the bite.

"Your lunch?" I asked, a harsh note to my tone.

"You're not jealous, are you?" Dante asked.

"Of course not," I said, far too quickly.

He grinned, as if he could sense the writhing, twisting sensation in my gut that felt an awful lot like jealousy.

"If I'd known you were visiting, I'd have held off," he said.

"I'm not food." I glanced at her. "She's not..."

"Oh, she's not dead. She's just enjoying the aftermath," he said.

Tingles formed low in my belly. I'd heard that vampire bites were like prolonged orgasms. It was one of the selling points for humans to pledge to their covens. I'd never spent a lot of time thinking about it since I'd never had a choice in where I went.

"Shall we?" Dante walked ahead, without waiting to see if I followed.

We were in the screened in room again, the bright afternoon light making the room much warmer than it had been last time I was here.

Dante settled on the same loveseat, taking up the whole thing with his long arms and legs. "So, why did the Crescent Pack send you to see me without my bidding?"

"Marcus is dead," I said.

His expression was stoic, completely unfazed by the name or by the fact that someone had died.

"You didn't kill him?" I asked.

He huffed out a laugh. "Is that why you're here? They think I murdered one of their own?"

"Nobody cares that he's dead," I clarified. "They thought maybe he was the one taking out the vampires. If that was true, it would mean no more killings."

"And it would tie everything up in a pretty little bow," he said.

"I guess so," I said. "So you didn't kill him?"

"I haven't killed anyone since the day I arrived in town." He grinned. "That might be a new streak for me."

"You killed that witch in the Council meeting," I reminded him.

"You're right. I guess I did." He shrugged. "But I didn't kill your shifter friends when they disrespected me. I had a feeling you might not like that."

I crossed my arms over my chest and glared at him. "Is that supposed to impress me or something?"

"Do you want me to impress you?" he asked.

I dropped my hands to my side. "Of course not. They just wanted me to tell you about Marcus."

"Was he involved in the lotus trade?" Dante asked.

"I don't think so. He could have been," I said. "He did other shady shit."

"Like?" he asked.

"Like kidnapping and selling shifters to other packs outside Lost Harbor," I said, the words making my stomach churn.

"Then I must say, I can see why nobody cares that he's dead," Dante said. "Why did they think it was me?"

"I guess cause they found one of the dead vampires at his place," I said. "The garage. Where you found us."

"That was his home?" Dante asked.

I nodded.

"Well, I can see the connection, then," he said. "But why not tell me of this suspicion sooner?"

"I don't know why they didn't tell you. They didn't bring it up at the Council meeting either," I said.

"Interesting," Dante said. "How'd he die?"

"Someone tore him to bits. Hung pieces of him from the trees." The words came out hollow and empty. I didn't feel even an ounce of sympathy for him.

Dante stood, and a flash of something dangerous sparked through those silver eyes. "In the trees?"

My brow furrowed. "That means something to you."

"I've seen it before," he admitted.

"What the fuck, Dante? Who the fuck is she?" A whiny female voice cut through the tension.

I spun to see the blonde, her neck caked in dried blood. Her mascara was running down her face and her lipstick was smeared across her mouth. It looked like there had been more than just feeding. Jealousy surged, making my insides feel hot and angry.

"Lily, darling, you were only ever just a snack." Dante's voice was as cold as ice.

"I let you have my blood," she hissed.

"You let anyone who asks have your blood." He turned away from her, his gaze fixed on me. "Go home, Lily."

Lily rested her hands on her hips. "I am the most

famous blood donor in Lost Harbor. I have fae blood in me, you know. Try finding that in another donor. You kick me out now; forget ever having a taste again."

Dante's smile was predatory, dangerous. A flicker of heat surged through me. Because clearly, I have issues.

Slowly, he turned to look at her again. "Leave my house or I'll make it so you can't give blood ever again. Do we understand each other?"

She made a squeaking sound, then scurried away. Her heels clacking over the ancient wood floors.

"I'm sorry about the interruption," he said. "Where were we?"

"You were about to tell me why you reacted to Marcus's body in the trees," I said.

He tensed, the muscles in his jaw feathering as he clenched and released. "Thank you for the information. Luke will take you home."

"I can find my own way home, thank you," I said.

"I said, Luke will take you home. You are mine, or have you forgotten? I don't want something bad to happen to my little spy," he said.

"You do know they're on to me. Henry pulled me from my job until this whole thing is done," I said. "They want to control what I see and hear."

"That makes your pack look very guilty," he said.

"For the attacks or the lotus?" I asked.

He shrugged.

"You needed me, boss?" Luke asked, appearing as if he'd been summoned.

I blinked a few times, trying not to show my unease.

"Take miss –" Dante cocked his head to the side, "I don't know your last name."

"Archer." Then I internally cursed for being so quick to answer. What was it with me around him?

I thought I saw his expression change, confusion or maybe even recognition, but it was so quick I couldn't be certain.

"Please take Miss Archer home." He turned and walked from the room.

"Is he always like this?" I asked, letting out an exasperated sigh.

Luke chuckled. "Nah. He usually doesn't play this nice."

"This is nice?" I asked.

Luke nodded. "You're still breathing and you have all your limbs. So, yeah, nice."

"Wonderful." I followed him to the car without another word. The sooner I was back in my apartment, where vampires couldn't follow without invitation, the better.

# CHAPTER
# TWENTY-ONE

Isla

My head throbbed, and I dreaded the thought of having to go back to work to face Henry. He'd basically given my job away and had sent me to look at a dead body. Did it still count as a dead body if it was in a dozen pieces?

Whatever. I was taking the rest of the day off.

"Hey, can you drop me at the Pearl?" I asked.

"Looking to do some day drinking?" Luke asked.

"I don't think that's any of your business," I said.

"It is when my boss told me to take you home," he said. "You're cute and all, but there's nothing worth pissing him off."

"You're not my type," I said.

"Sweetie, I haven't been with a female in a century and I ain't about to start now," he said.

"Okay, I appreciate that. But can you please just drop me there? My roommate works there and I don't exactly feel like going home to an empty apartment," I said.

He was silent for a moment, as if he was considering my words. "That sounds safer. I'll let the boss know I dropped you there."

"He's not my boss," I said.

"If you say so, sweetie. But last I saw, he was giving you orders, and having me drive you around. You didn't see that blood bag getting a ride in his personal car, did you?" Luke pointed out.

"I'm not doing this by choice," I said.

"Are you trying to convince me or convince yourself?" He stopped the car.

I didn't bother giving him an answer. At this point, I wasn't even sure. All I knew was that I was getting really, really tired of other people telling me what to do. "Thanks for the ride."

"See you soon," he said.

I closed the door and didn't bother to turn back and wave. The last thing I needed was a vampire thinking I was his friend. Or any of the shifters thinking I'd changed sides.

Considering that it was the middle of the day, the Pearl was packed. I passed tables full of shifters and made my way to the bar, grabbing an empty stool between Josiah Mack and Adam Parker.

Josiah was a cop, and I noticed that he had a soda in front of him instead of a beer. Adam, on the other hand, was on at least his second beer based on the empty glass in front of him. Thankfully, both males were engaged in conversation with others, so they didn't even acknowledge me when I sat.

Maddie was behind the bar, busy pouring drinks and typing orders into the computer. It took a minute before she noticed me, but her whole face lit up when she saw me.

"What are you doing here?" She set her elbows on the bar and leaned over. "Henry actually let you leave for a real lunch break?"

"He replaced me," I said.

Her eyes widened. "You were fired?"

I shook my head. "I don't think so. He said he wants me to focus on the vampire thing. As if it's an actual thing and not just some stupid power trip between two alpha males."

"Vampire thing?" Josiah said, turning in my direction. "I heard about that. You're the new snitch."

"I'm not a snitch," I said.

He snorted. "You agreed to it, didn't you?"

"You say that like I had a choice," I snapped.

"You always have a choice," he said.

"I don't have healing powers or long life, in case you forgot," I said.

"I'd rather be dead than be some vamp's blood bag," he said.

I lifted my chin and turned my head from side to side. "See any bite marks? I'm not a blood bag. I'm doing what the alpha of the Crescent Pack asked me to do. If you have a problem with it, take it up with him."

"There are other places to bite someone," he said.

"Fuck you, Josiah," Maddie said. "You have no idea what it's like to be a human in this world. Until you've been the vulnerable one, you can shut the fuck up."

Josiah shoved his plate toward Maddie. "If you're going to serve vampire groupies here, you can kiss my business goodbye."

"So long, asshole," Maddie said.

Josiah stood, a scowl on his face. "Don't bother calling us for help when those vamps turn on you."

"Like I said, talk to Henry. This isn't my choice."

"Right." He walked away, and I was left with my pulse racing and a feeling of shame settling over me. I knew the risks of being involved with a vampire, but I didn't think following Henry's orders would have this kind of backlash.

"Is he telling the truth?" Adam asked.

I turned to face the huge shifter. "What's it to you?" My tone was cutting and I might regret it, but I was so tired of feeling helpless and out of control.

He leaned in and sniffed. I tensed. "Do you mind?"

"You do smell like vampires." He shrugged. "Good for you. Fuck who you want, girl."

"I'm not fucking a vampire," I said.

"Maybe you should," Adam said. "Everyone knows the wolves treat you like shit. You've always been too good for this place."

My brow furrowed. I never knew he even noticed me.

Maddie's hand rested on mine. "That's what I always tell her. You seeing anyone, Adam? She and Ryder broke up."

"Maddie!" I hissed.

"Bout time," Adam said. "And I'm flattered, but I'm afraid I'm off the market."

"Of course you are," Maddie said. "I hadn't heard and usually the bartender knows. I'm hurt."

He laughed. "Mating bond. Last week. I'm still processing."

"Oh?" Maddie poured another beer, then set it in front of him. "You don't sound happy."

"She's not what I expected," he said. "But we'll figure it out."

"Leave the man alone," I scolded. "Let him drink and think. And while you're at it, how about a big-ass margarita?"

Maddie grinned. "You got it, girl."

I kept pace with Adam. He knocked back the beer and Maddie kept my margaritas coming. We talked about everything but love while we shared a few appetizers. For the first time in a long time, I forgot about work and my plans for the future. It felt mundane and freeing. Sure, it was probably because of all the booze, but every so often, maybe that was what was needed.

Maddie's shift was nearing its end, and I had switched to water. Not that it did much to dilute the tequila that was making me giggle at everything. "Give me a few minutes to check out," Maddie said. "Then we'll go."

I waved as she headed to the kitchen to drop her cash register tray and dump her apron in the hamper. When she walked back out, her expression was stormy.

"What's wrong?" I asked.

"Shirley called in. Ned needs me to stay. I'm so sorry. You need me to call you a cab?" Maddie asked. "Or I can call Kaylie. I'm sure she'd come get you."

"My mate is on her way," Adam said. "We can give you a ride."

Through my foggy brain, I assessed his words. Normally, accepting a ride home from a bar with a man you barely knew while drunk was a hard no. But he was a mated wolf. That was pretty much about as loyal as you could get. Plus, his mate was the one driving, not him.

"Alright," I said. "Thanks, Adam. You know, we should hang out more often."

Adam clapped me on the back. "You're like one of my best friends now, Isla."

"I know, right?" The booze made me feel euphoric, and I found myself wondering why we weren't friends before today.

"I'm sure your mate is going to love that," Maddie said. "Maybe I should call you a cab."

"She'll be fine," Adam said. "She knows I literally can't even look at another woman. So what if I never asked for a mating bond? So what if I never wanted to be bound to one woman for the rest of my life? It's not like I get a choice. That's it. It's done. Forever."

"See? It'll be fine," I slurred.

"Adam? You ready?" A female voice called.

I turned to see a stunning red-head. Her face was dusted with freckles and her blue eyes were like pools of water. "Adam, you didn't tell me she was a fucking goddess."

"Yeah, she is," Maddie agreed.

The red-head frowned. "Who is this?"

"This is my new best friend, Isla," Adam said proudly.

I stood, swaying on my feet. "Nice to meet you."

"You two are sloshed," she said. "It's four in the afternoon."

"And I already saw a dead body and sassed off to a vampire. What a productive day," I said.

Red rolled her eyes. "Come on, Adam. Let's get you home to a cup of coffee."

"I promised Isla a ride," Adam said. "Can we do that, baby-doll?"

She folded her arms across her chest.

"I swear, she's harmless," Maddie said.

"I am definitely harmless," I agreed.

"I was going to drive her home, but my boss is making me stay," Maddie added.

"Fine, come on," Red said.

Adam and I giggled our way to the car. I could tell his mate didn't like me, but that was her problem. Adam was great. No wonder he wasn't happy with his bond. She was a total stick in the mud.

The car was nice. Leather seats and a huge sunroof. I hadn't been in a car this nice before.

"Where do you live?" Red asked.

I gave her my cross streets, then fidgeted with the seatbelt. I couldn't get it to work, so I stopped trying and just leaned back against the soft leather. The booze was making things a little uneven, and I felt a bit woozy. The longer the drive, the more I remembered why I rarely let myself drink this much.

When we pulled up to my apartment, I was barely out the door before the car sped off. "I don't think Adam's mate likes me." There was nobody around, so I was talking to myself. And that's when I realized that maybe I had too much to drink.

Working to steady my vision, I focused my steps, one in front of the other, until I reached my apartment. As soon as I flipped on the light, I jumped.

I wasn't alone.

# CHAPTER
# TWENTY-TWO

Isla

Dante studied me, his eyes scanning my body before locking his gaze on mine. "You're unharmed."

"You're in my apartment," I said, fighting against the uneasy feeling of not being in full control. I was seriously regretting those margaritas. "Fucking Maddie." I loved my best friend, I did, but how stupid could you be? Everyone knew not to let in a vampire.

He stood, his movements smooth and graceful. His expression was hard and intense. "Where is Luke?"

My brow furrowed. "Luke dropped me off at the Pearl." I shook my head. "Wait, don't change the subject. You can't be in my apartment. I didn't invite you in, and if my roommate did, it shouldn't count."

"Nobody invited me," he said.

"Then how are you in my apartment?" I demanded. "And why are you here?"

"After you refused to let me in, I took matters into my own hands." He smirked. "Your landlord was more than happy to accept a generous cash offer for the building."

"You bought the building?" I felt dizzy. Unsteady on my own feet, I made it to the couch and plopped down.

Dante's nose wrinkled. "You smell like a distillery."

"Well, I needed a way to numb everything after today," I said. "Thanks for killing my vibe."

"It's not a vibe, it's irresponsible. What if someone else had been here instead of me?" He sat down next to me on the couch and my body instantly reacted to him.

In a horny kind of way.

I was never drinking tequila again.

"Nobody should be in my apartment," I said. "You certainly shouldn't."

"I had to check on you," he said.

"How many times do I have to tell you, there's nothing going on between us," I said.

"Luke didn't return after he dropped you off," he said.

That helped sober me up. "What?"

"I suppose it was a matter of time before one of my own was targeted by the killer," he said.

I leaped from the couch. "We have to find him."

"Anna is already looking for him. Besides, since when do you care about vampires?" he asked.

"I don't want anyone to die," I said. "Is that what you

think about me? You think that I'm that hateful? I don't have anything against vampires in general."

He leaned in until we were inches from each other. "So, it's personal. It's just me you don't like."

I could smell him. That cedar and honey scent was intoxicating. I wanted to bottle it and spray it on my clothes.

Swallowing hard, I scooted away, giving more space between the two of us. "I told you. I belong to the shifters."

He smiled, his fangs gleaming. "You belong to me."

His mouth was on me and before I could talk myself out of it, I kissed him back.

Kissing him felt right and wrong, but I couldn't wrap my head around the logic of why it would be so wrong. I needed more of him.

My fingers toyed with the hem of his shirt before sliding underneath. His skin was surprisingly warm against my palms. He groaned, his hands gripping my ass.

And then I hiccupped.

My eyes widened, and I pulled away from the kiss. Another hiccup. I covered my mouth with my hand, embarrassment searing me from the inside out.

I hiccupped again.

Then I burst out laughing.

Dante smiled and shook his head. His hand brushed away the hair that had fallen in front of my eyes. "You had too much to drink."

"No, I'm fine." *Hiccup.*

"You're drunk," he said.

"So? Why do you care if I'm drunk," I said.

He kissed my forehead, then stood. "I'm going to go."

I grabbed his wrist. "Stay and do all the naughty things you want to do to me."

He winced and groaned as if in pain. "You have no idea how badly I want to."

"Then do," I said. "Show me why you're so fucking cocky."

He grabbed a handful of my hair and yanked my face to his. I let out a startled yelp.

"Next time I fuck you, you're going to be fully aware. You'll know exactly who I am and exactly what you're asking for. Then I'm going to make you beg." He released my hair, and I fell against the back of the couch, breathless, clit throbbing with need.

"Don't invite anyone else in here. Just because I own the place doesn't mean that other vampires can come in," he said.

I wasn't sure how long I stared at the closed door after he left, his words haunting me. If he hadn't stopped us, I'd have done anything he wanted.

The worst part was that I was disappointed.

I needed a shower. And some coffee. And I was never drinking again.

By the time I turned off the shower, most of the tequila had worn off. The reality of what I'd said and done with the vampire king hit me like a blow to the chest. His words reverberated in my mind, sending both terror and desire coursing through my veins.

What the fuck was I doing?

I was already walking a tightrope as it was. Giving in to the desire I felt for him would be knocking me off, and there wasn't a net to catch me.

The fact that I was even interested in him was a whole other problem. I'd watched him kill without remorse. I'd watched how he dismissed the woman he'd fed from.

And there was that. The fact that he needed to drink blood to survive. I didn't care how pleasurable it was supposed to be. I was not going to be someone's meal.

My phone rang. Figuring it would be Maddie, I grabbed it, answering without looking at the screen. "Hey, you on your way?"

"Do I have some competition?" Dante asked.

My brow furrowed. "Why are you calling me?"

"Just making sure you didn't pass out. I hear humans can't handle their liquor well," he said.

"I'm hanging up," I replied.

"Sleep well." The line went dead.

I groaned, annoyed that he'd been the first one to hang up. I didn't even want to know how he got my number or why he thought it was a good idea to call me. He was going to get me killed.

GINA WAS ALREADY in my office when I arrived. The shades were down and my sunny space was like a tomb. I glared at her. "You're in my chair."

"Henry says you're to go see him." She flipped her hair, then smiled at me.

Annoyance made my muscles tense. I hadn't believed he'd actually follow through with the threat to replace me. There was no way she was able to handle the work for the pack, but that wasn't my problem. At least not right now. I was likely going to have to clean up after her, but I didn't have a choice.

I walked over to the window and opened the blinds, filling the space with light. Several of my plants were already sagging. They looked like they'd been neglected for weeks. This was why I was a believer in talking to plants. "They need watered. Don't over water them and kill them or I will take it out on you."

Gina squealed, her eyes wide. "What the fuck, Isla?"

"I'm serious, Gina." I didn't know where this was coming from, but there were few things that were good about my life. The cozy office full of green things was one of them. I did not want to come back to a sea of dead plants when Henry realized Gina couldn't cut it.

"Alright, I'll water them," she said.

"Keep the window open." I didn't wait for a response before I left.

On my walk over to Henry's office, I realized it wasn't Gina I was mad at. I was furious with Henry, angry with Dante, and pissed at myself. Everything I'd worked so hard for was suddenly hanging in the balance. This was not my plan. I needed things to go back the way they were.

Henry wasn't alone in his office, but I didn't mask my irritation when I walked in. "You're seriously going to have her do my job?"

"I told you I was," he said. "You know I always keep my word." He turned to the shifters gathered around his desk. I recognized Derek and Killian, but there were two I wasn't familiar with. I caught the edges of a tattoo peeking under the sleeve of one of them. It looked an awful lot like the tattoo the tiger shifters wore.

"Everyone out. I need a word with Isla," Henry said.

The room cleared quickly, and I was suddenly alone with Henry. I'd been alone with him before, but I don't think it had ever been in his office. He had a desk and table surrounded by chairs in addition to a few book shelves surprisingly full of books. But as soon as the others left, the space suddenly felt too small.

"What happened yesterday?" Henry asked.

"Which part?" I asked.

"Start at the beginning," he said.

*Shit.* He was going to bust me for not coming back after I went to Dante's. "You told me you were giving my job away. I was upset."

"Is that why you had the vampire king at your apartment? *Inside* your apartment?" Henry's tone was flat and emotionless. I'd heard him speak like this in the past. Usually before he lost his shit.

I opened my mouth to explain and then closed it when

I realized what he was saying. He was pissed I had a vampire in my house, but that meant he'd had someone watching me. "You're spying on me?"

"You are Crescent Pack property, and I sent you in alone to see the vampire king. I sent a guy to check on you," he said. "Imagine his surprise when he watched that blood sucker walk out of your apartment."

"You're the one who told me to do whatever it took," I hissed.

"So you're fucking him?"

"I am not and if I was, it would be exactly what you expected from me, wouldn't it?" I asked.

"Let me make something very clear. You are not above the rules. Fraternizing with a vampire is considered treason."

"I know that. And if you think I'd be willing to sell my body for information, you don't know me at all," I said.

He stood and walked around the desk, leaning against the side. "Why was he there?"

"He bought the building so he could go inside without my invitation," I said.

He lifted a brow. "He bought a building in our territory?"

"Isn't it all *his* territory?" I shouldn't have said it, but I was pissed. Henry wasn't any better than Dante. These males were throwing my life around like it was worthless. They didn't care what the consequences were for a human.

"Once it was," he said. "But they've been gone too long. The Council doesn't want to let go of the power."

"The Council or you?" I asked.

"Don't push it, Isla," he said. "There's a witness that he was at your place."

"None of this would be happening if you hadn't made me do this," I pointed out.

"Then prove your loyalty. Get me some dirt on this guy. Help me figure out why he's here, what he's after. And help me figure out a way to get him to leave," Henry said.

"I don't think I'm going to be able to do that," I said. "He's trying to use me for the same purpose."

"Then you're going to have to play him. Lie. Tell him what he wants to hear so you can earn his trust," Henry said.

"I'm not sleeping with him," I said.

"Even if you don't, everyone already thinks you have," he said. "Get me something good."

I stood.

"Where are you going?" Henry asked.

"Isn't this my job now? Spying for you?" I asked.

He grunted. "I need something by the end of the week, Isla. The Council is breathing down my neck."

"Got it, boss," I said.

On my way out of his office, I wondered what the hell I was going to do. I had some information I could give Henry. Dante was after information about lotus, but I wasn't sure I trusted Henry enough to bring that up. I couldn't trust anyone right now.

This was bigger than me. I wasn't sure if Marcus was the lead Dante was after, or if the Crescent Pack was directly involved. Until I could find out something about lotus on my own, I couldn't say anything to either male. I needed to know exactly what I was getting into.

That meant I had to pay a visit to the last person I wanted to see: my mother.

# CHAPTER
# TWENTY-THREE

Isla

My mom lived in my grandmother's old house. We'd moved in after my grandmother died and my mom quickly turned it from a place of refuge, to a place I needed to escape. I'd tried to keep the green house running, but I was young, and with school and other responsibilities, it fell to the wayside.

My feet crunched across the gravel driveway. I breathed in the scent of lilacs and glanced toward the abandoned greenhouse. Most of the glass had been shattered, but it was overgrown with vines and flowers. At least the plants were retaking the space even without my care.

I walked past the lilac bushes near the entry to the house and paused a moment to observe the fuzzy bees zooming around the flowers. At least there were some remnants of my grandmother's love for all things that grew.

My mom hadn't taken care of any of it, but the hardy plants thrived on their own. The similarity between my own childhood and these now wild plants wasn't lost on me. I was never hungry. At least there was always food in the house. That was about it. If I got to school, it was because I got myself up and there. The day I turned thirteen, my mom decided I was too much work and told me to pack. I missed school that day because I was dropped off at the Crescent Pack's home for girls.

I spent the next three years living in a communal space until I was able to demonstrate that my skills were worth something to the alpha. I finished high school and worked every evening for the alpha to earn enough to cover rent in a run-down shoebox of an apartment. When Maddie asked about sharing a place, I jumped on it. It was a major upgrade from what I'd been able to afford on my own.

It took me two years before I trusted Maddie enough to consider her a friend. Until her, I hadn't known what it was like to have someone who gave a shit about you since my grandmother's death.

I frowned at the cascading memories, shoving them away as I knocked on the door.

This was why I didn't come here. Most of the time, I could ignore my past. When I came here, it poured into my mind like water breaking through a dam.

The door swung open and a naked male shifter

answered. His gut hung out, covering him enough to block the parts I absolutely did not want to see. Okay, that was a lie, I didn't want to see any of him. Dark hair covered every inch of him and he looked like he hadn't shaved in a few days. It wasn't sexy stubble or a nice beard. Rather that in between phase. Food was stuck in the whiskers.

"Who are you?" he demanded.

"I'm here to see Cheryl," I said.

"She's busy," he said.

"How is she busy if you're here and not in her bedroom?" I asked.

"I was getting a snack," he said.

"Who's there, Frank?" my mom called.

"It's Isla," I said.

"Let her in, Frank," my mom said.

Frank hesitated, then moved aside enough for me to see my mom approach. She had the same brown hair I had, only hers was streaked with blonde highlights. Her too-thin arm reached out to shove Frank aside. "Move, ya big lug."

"My time isn't up," Frank said.

"Go wait in the bedroom. I'll be there soon," she said. "Besides, you haven't paid me for last week's session yet, so maybe you shouldn't be bitching to me."

Frank grumbled, but he turned. I was not prepared for the flat, blinding white ass. It was covered with just as much hair as the rest of his body. I winced, and turned my attention to my mom. "You can do better," I whispered.

"I heard that," Frank said just before he closed the door.

"I *can* do better, and you better not forget that," my mom shouted. She turned her attention to me. "Come in, Isla."

I followed her into the living room and took a seat on the old blue couch. I could feel the springs under my ass. Nothing had changed except for everything looking more worn and dirty.

My mom took a seat in the rocking chair across from me. She smiled, wrinkles forming near her eyes when she did. "How are you, darling?"

"I'm alright, ma, how are you doing?"

"I'm good. Things are steady." She looked fifty years older than the last time I saw her. Her thin figure was positively bony now. She looked like she hadn't eaten a good meal in months. Her hair looked dull and her hazel eyes, my eyes, looked flat and empty.

How long had it been since I saw her? Only a couple of months. How had she changed so much in such a short time?

I glanced around the room, noticing the baggie on the coffee table. The blue powder was unmistakable. I grabbed it and held it up. "Mom?"

I'd come expecting to ask for some information since my mom was more connected to the human population here, but I hadn't considered that she'd be using the substance herself. "When did this start?"

"Oh, sweetie, I've been using lotus for a while. It's so much safer than the stuff I did when you were living with me." She said it as if that made it okay.

I couldn't go there with her. Nothing I'd ever said had been enough for her. I'd never been enough. Every time I did stop by to visit, she acted as if nothing bad had passed between us. It was enough to make me question my own sanity.

"Where do you get it, mom?" I asked. That's what I'd come for, anyway. I needed more information about this stuff before I moved forward with talking to either Henry or Dante.

I knew they were both the bad guy. But I just needed to survive here until I could leave. Whichever side was going to get me there, was where I had to go. I didn't like the thought of siding with the vampires. It was dangerous. Probably more dangerous than being more open with Henry. But Dante had more power. If he chose to step up to the title he held, he could wipe out the pack without a second thought.

I was pretty sure I was fucked either way.

Her brow furrowed. "I thought you weren't into these things?"

"I'm not," I said.

"Then why do you want to know where it comes from?" she asked. "You've judged me for my choices your entire life. You and my mom. The two of you, thick as thieves; looking down your noses at me."

"Are you kidding me? I was a child. You are my mother.

You shouldn't have been doing things that made me judge you." The words just tumbled out.

She rose to her feet. "Go ahead. Make me the villain. I'm a terrible mother. I know it. You know it."

I stood. "You were a terrible mother, but that's not why I'm here."

"Then why, Isla? Why are you here if not to dig up the ghosts of the past?" she demanded.

I blew out a breath while I considered how to word my questions. I'd mostly forgiven her long ago. Well, maybe not forgiven, but I'd let it go. She wasn't going to change. She wasn't the maternal type, but when she forgot to take the tonic one month, she ended up with me.

At least she'd been in love with my father. That helped. I used to imagine what my life might have been like had my father not died when I was a baby. Maybe she'd be happy now. Maybe I'd have grown up in a loving family.

There was no changing the past. Only dealing with surviving my present so I could have a future far from the dysfunction of this place.

"I have a friend who got into something she shouldn't have," I said. "I'm trying to help her find a way out. It's better if I don't tell you all the details."

She lifted a brow. "She got involved with lotus?"

I nodded.

"Cheryl, what the fuck is taking so long?" The bedroom door opened and the naked shifter peeked out. "I've got to be at work in an hour."

My mom's shoulders tensed and I caught the slightest

twitch of her upper lip. Then she fixed a smile on her face and flipped her hair over her shoulder as she turned to look at her client. "Give me one minute and then I'll make it worth the wait." Her tone was seductive, her lips in a perfectly practiced pout.

Watching her go from my mom to seductress was always one of the strangest things about growing up with her. She was capable of being so many different people. She had a mask for every client. The only mask she never perfected was that of a loving parent.

"I get mine from Tico next door," she said. "But I heard a rumor that most of it is run out of Jack's Bar."

"That place is still open?" The bar existed in a weird little patch of land that protruded into shifter territory and hadn't been claimed by anyone. It acted as a sort of neutral bar that any creature could get to. They risked trouble for passing through other territories to get there, but once there, they were untouchable. It was like international waters.

"Still run by Baron?" I asked.

She nodded.

"Why would a bar run by a vampire help push lotus?" While lotus could kill any supernatural, it was instantly lethal to vampires. It didn't make sense that a vampire run bar would assist in pushing something.

My mom chuckled. "Since when did Baron have any kind of moral compass?"

"Good point," I said. If the runners were paying him for the use of the bar, he probably didn't care.

It wasn't much different than what the Crescent Pack did. While I would like to think that Henry didn't approve of what people like Marcus did, they ignored the moral and ethical sides and just took their cut.

Fucking supernaturals.

"Chery!" the male shifter bellowed.

"I should go," she said.

"Yeah, thanks for the information," I said.

"Whatever you have planned, be careful."

"I will," I said, ignoring the way my stomach tightened at her false concern. Where was that concern for me as a child when I needed it most? It didn't matter now. I wasn't going to be here much longer. I would be able to finally push away my past trauma and fully move on.

My throat tightened at the thought that this might be the last time I saw her. I didn't stop by often and she'd never once checked in on me. "Take care of yourself, ma."

She nodded, her expression sad. I wondered if she knew that one of these visits would be my last. For a moment, I thought maybe she cared a little.

"Some of my clients were asking about you," she said. "If you ever change jobs, I can send them your way."

All good thoughts gone. She knew I didn't want to follow her footsteps. "Bye, mom."

I watched as she walked to the bedroom and closed the door behind her. I let myself out, then let my feet lead me to the destroyed green house.

The floral scent of the lilacs lingered in the background, mingling with the scent of decay and devil's trumpets. My feet crunched over the remains of broken glass and I took in the crumbling and rotting wood counters. Dirt and debris coated every surface. Most of the plants weren't what we'd planted in here. Wildflowers and weeds had grown in their place.

Moving forward, I looked at the back where she'd taken such care to grow the night blooming devil's trumpets. There were still healthy plants, surviving despite their odds.

A lump rose in my throat. I could relate.

I knew better than to touch the toxic flowers, but I wished I had a watering can to care for them. It was nice to see some of them here, thriving without my grandmother's expert hands.

The blooms were closed now, but they'd open later in the day. They were dangerous plants, not what they seemed. Sleeping during the day, awaking at night. Every part of them was poisonous, despite their appearance.

There was something about that thought that resonated with me. Nobody expected anything from me. As a human, I was ignored, dismissed. I wasn't seen as a threat. Usually, that bothered me. It made me feel weak. But I realized it was exactly the reason both Henry and Dante had asked for my help. Nobody would suspect me. I could go places they couldn't.

Their problem was that they also underestimated me. They thought they could control me and get me to play their games.

I was going to play both of them until I could find out which one would help me stay alive.

No more shrinking human. It was my time to bloom.

# CHAPTER
# TWENTY-FOUR

Isla

Jack's Bar was nearly empty when I arrived. A bartender was cleaning glasses behind the bar as if I'd walked into an old western film.

All the windows were painted black, making the place feel more like a tomb than a building. The walls were covered in maps, wanted posters, and scribbles written in marker. A few walls were spray painted with symbols that were partially covered with whatever was pinned on top of them. It was decades of patrons adding to the walls, making it look like a strange collage. A couple of arrows and a few daggers stuck from the walls in the back. I wondered if they had been added for aesthetics or if they'd missed their intended target and been left behind.

At a corner table, I caught sight of two large males

who were probably shifters based on their build. In another corner, a pair of fae were drinking sparkling green fairy wine out of champagne glasses. Their long fair hair and pointed ears easily giving them away. They looked out of place in the dim and dirty bar.

A male with long black hair that hung in curtains in front of his face, sat on a stool at the scuffed up bar. Dirty hands with long fingernails were wrapped around a glass. I was pretty sure the splotches on his clothing were dried blood.

"What can I get you?" the bartender asked.

I could feel the eyes of the other patrons on me as I crossed to the bar. I took a stool on the opposite end from the bloody patron. "Vodka and soda, please."

He grunted in response, then got to work making my drink. A moment later, he slid it across the surface and I quickly took a sip. The vodka burned my throat on its way down. It was pretty much all vodka. Well, that explained why people would go out of their way to come here. The pour was more than generous, but it was also dangerous. I had a much lower tolerance for alcohol than the supernatural creatures I lived with.

"Why don't you join us for a drink, little one?" A honey-sweet voice called.

I glanced over at the smiling fae male. He was gorgeous. Every inch the temptation he was crafted to be. It really wasn't fair how beautiful all the creatures here were. Monsters disguised to look like angels.

The fae's violet eyes practically glittered. He lifted his

champagne glass and the feral smile didn't reach his eyes. "We promise we won't bite."

Right. But one sip of that fairy wine and I'd do anything he asked. No, thank you. "I need some alone time right now." I smiled politely, resisting the urge to thank him. At least I'd been taught those basic survival skills. Never, ever, thank a fae. They'd take it as a favor owed and they'd make you pay.

The male inclined his head, then turned back to his companion. I blew out a slow breath, then took another sip of my drink.

"Smart girl," the bloody male said without turning to me.

I wasn't sure exactly what kind of creature he was, but I hoped that ignoring him was the best option. Focusing on my drink, I kept my gaze ahead, watching the bartender find things to wipe down. He looked like he might be human. I didn't see fangs. He wasn't bulky like most shifters, and he didn't have pointed ears. He might be a witch, or he could be something else.

There were so many other creatures hidden and living among the supernaturals here. Since I was basically locked away in shifter territory, my knowledge wasn't as vast as I'd like. I heard stories, but I rarely interacted with anyone who wasn't wolf shifter or human.

The sound of the door opening had the bartender looking up. He physically responded to whomever had walked in. His shoulders tensed and he grimaced briefly before making a show of organizing liquor bottles.

The sound of heels clicked across the floor, and the newcomer took the stool next to me. I cringed. Of-fucking-course. I pretended to sip my drink while I let my eyes flick over to see who had joined me.

The woman was petite and curvy. With dark brown hair and thick lashes. Her makeup was impeccable and her tight red dress belonged in a club, not a run-down bar. "Vodka martini, dry, two olives."

The drink was delivered by the time she had the words out. She must be a regular. Her eyes found mine, and she smirked as she took a long pull from the drink, downing half the glass in a single gulp.

She set the glass on the scuffed up bar. "What brings you here, sunshine?"

"Avoiding reality," I said.

"It's about the only place us humans can do that," she said.

"Tell me about it," I replied.

She fished out the olive and popped it in her mouth. "You solo, or did they sell you off to one of the houses?"

"Crescent Pack," I said.

"I used to belong to the vampires." She held up her arm, and I noticed all the scars along her skin.

"You got out?" I took a sip of my drink to try to hide my surprise.

She grinned. "I can help you get out, too."

Alarm bells blared, but I pressed forward. I already had a way out. Fully paid for and ready to go. But my curiosity was piqued. "Oh?"

She tossed back the rest of her drink, then slammed it on the counter. She grabbed the second olive, holding it between her finger and thumb. "It's not for the faint of heart."

Her glass was replaced by a fresh one and she dropped the olive into it before picking it up. "It takes a special kind of human to go against the order of things in this town. But it can be done."

"How'd you do it?" I asked.

She leaned in so close I could smell the vodka on her breath. She whispered, "Lotus."

My eyes widened. This was what I'd come here for, but I didn't think it would find me. "You have a connection?"

"I distribute for a guy, yeah," she said. "He's always looking for more ways to funnel it into new territories. You'd have very little competition. It's not being sold in the Crescent Pack territory yet."

"It's not?" That was a surprise. I knew it was a newer drug, and that it wasn't as widespread as others, but I figured it would find its way everywhere. Especially since it had been at my mom's house. She was under Crescent Pack protection. Though, she wasn't owned by them the way I was. She worked for them, paid dues like everyone else.

"They have to come here to pick up their fix. They might sell it secondhand, but you'd get it direct. No mark up. Pretty little thing like you could make a killing if you played your cards right," she said.

I didn't want to sound too eager, but I was curious to

see how far I could get with this. It didn't sound like the Crescent Pack was involved, but who was, then? And why did Dante care?

"I might be interested in learning more," I said.

She smiled, then turned toward the bartender, who was trying to look like he wasn't listening to every word. "Another round for my new friend. On my tab."

He nodded, then a second drink appeared in front of me. The woman lifted her martini glass in a toast. "To new friendships and freedom. Us humans have to look out for each other. Gods know nobody else will."

I lifted my glass and clinked it against hers. My stomach tightened as a mixture of guilt and nerves tangled within. She was right. None of the supernaturals cared about us. I didn't feel guilt for working independently of Henry or Dante. I felt bad about using this woman to gain information when I had no interest in working for her boss.

"Cheers," I said. "To friendship and freedom."

She sipped her drink, a smile on her ruby lips. "I like you, and I think my boss will be interested in making your acquaintance."

I finished my first drink, then sipped on the second. My head feeling a little woozy already. I hadn't eaten in a while and the liquor was going right to my head. "Why wait?"

She knocked back her second drink. "My kind of girl. We'll take my car."

I took another sip, then left the rest of the drink on the

counter. Thankfully, she didn't press. The buzz of the liquor had me feeling a little more brave than I probably should, and I could tell I wasn't thinking as clearly as usual. But what did I have to lose?

Even though I didn't want to admit it to myself, I was already facing the possibility of death with the game I was thrust into. I might as well move forward on my terms.

I followed the woman away from the bar.

"Wrong choice," the bloody male called after me.

I ignored him again, but I did wonder if I might be heading toward something more dangerous than the shit I was already involved with.

"I'm May," she said as she started the engine.

"Isla," I replied.

"Isla, I'm about to change your life."

# CHAPTER
# TWENTY-FIVE

Isla

THE LONGER I was in the car, the heavier the weight of what I'd done grew in the pit of my stomach. I was smarter than this. There was a reason I was still alive after growing up in the Crescent Pack. A reason I had avoided some of the pitfalls that other women suffered. I didn't do things like this. I used reason and logic. I listened to my gut.

Apparently, my gut was easily swayed when I had to choose between a pair of alpha males and a human woman. I'd initially thought that May was the lesser of the evils, but I should know more than anyone how deceiving appearances can be.

Sure, I'd had my share of beatings and abuse, but that was mostly from other kids or the occasional adult at the pack house. This was a whole other level of stupid.

Internally kicking myself, I kept my attention out the window so I could memorize each turn we made. "Where exactly is this friend of yours?"

"Oh, he's not my friend. He's my boss. And he's a monster. But he's better than the monsters I grew up with," she said.

"The vampires?" It was impolite to press, but the scars weren't hidden. Mine were, making it harder to see that I'd suffered in my own way.

"Mm-hmm." She glanced at me. "They can turn it off, you know. The bliss. That thing that makes feeding feel good."

My chest constricted. "I'm sorry."

"I know you are. I can see it in your eyes. You're looking for an escape, a way out. Did you know we all have a price attached to us?"

"I'm not sure what you mean," I said.

"There's a way out of your contract with the shifters. That was how the Council got the whole bullshit of owning us humans passed. There's always a loophole," she said.

"There's not for me. Trust me, I've looked," I said.

"So you're saving to leave town, then," she said matter-of-factly. "That's ballsy. Good for you."

I didn't respond. How had she seen right through me so quickly? Not even my best friend, who I lived with, knew what I was planning.

"This'll help," she said. "You get paid well, and he

doesn't beat us. As long as you give him the money for the product, he leaves you alone."

"Don't you feel bad about it, though? Contributing to more human suffering?" I asked.

She chuckled. "Am I, though? Most humans won't leave here. They need a way to cope. Lotus is totally safe for humans. Kills vampires and harms other supernaturals. It's safer than alcohol. We might as well enjoy something for a change," she said.

"You've tried it?" I asked.

"Sure. Twice. I don't like the way it makes me feel. Too out of control. I like to be present in my body," she said.

"Two martinis present?" I winced. "Sorry, that was super judgy."

"I started drinking when I was twelve to numb the pain," she said. "It takes a whole lot more than two martinis to get me there."

"I thought I had it bad," I said.

"I've made my peace," she said. "And I have my reasons for staying. So here I am, pushing lotus to other pathetic humans who are too stupid or too traumatized to make a change."

"How many are there like you?" I asked.

"If you're wondering about competition, you're in luck. There aren't a lot of us doing this yet, and there's none approved to sell in Crescent territory. It's the one place no human seems to want to touch," she said.

We were driving through a warehouse complex near the docks. The bright light of the late afternoon sun cast long shadows over the nearly empty parking lot. "We're in vampire territory."

"We are," she said. "Best place to hide something from vampires is right under their cold, dead noses." Her grin was savage. I could tell she enjoyed the sense of revenge she got by selling something that would kill those who used to torture her.

I can't say I blamed her. I'd pushed a lot of my past away so I didn't have to dwell on it. That was impossible when those hurting you were digging their fangs into you and taking your blood.

The car stopped in front of an unassuming warehouse. It was beige, just like the others around it. Two large bay doors were closed and a smaller door for people to walk through was next to those. I made a note that it was numbered as twenty-seven above the door.

The warehouse was teeming with activity. Long tables were lined with piles of blue powder in huge bags. Workers sliced bags open and scooped the lotus into smaller bags, weighing each one on a scale, before sealing them up.

I had to remind myself to close my mouth. When May said she was taking me to meet someone, I didn't think she'd take me directly to the source.

It seemed like an impossible amount of lotus. Lost Harbor wasn't that large. Where was it all going? As far as I knew, it was mostly humans who used the blue powder. But this was far more than they'd need, even if every human in the city was using daily.

"Impressive, isn't it?" May asked.

"I didn't realize they needed so much," I said.

"It's been the hub of operations for a couple of months now. When I first started, it was imported, but then human law enforcement started to crack down on it."

"This is way more than they need here," I said.

She nodded. "Yep. It's enough for most of the demand in the whole country. Human and supernatural cities. Though we'll have to expand again soon. Every week, we run out."

"Wow." I stared at the operation in awe. The workers moved in flawless rhythm. Each one practiced in their duties. There were at least a hundred people working with the product and I caught sight of others walking around as if monitoring the process.

The whole thing didn't look a few months old. It looked established and well-run. I couldn't even get the shifters at the pack house to throw out the empty bottles of creamer instead of putting them back in the fridge.

"Come on, I want you to meet him," she said.

*Him.* Whoever ran this whole thing. Nervous flutters filled my chest, but I remained focused on my goal. I needed to know how this was all connected. Was Marcus part of this? Was the lotus trade connected to the dead vampires?

The timeline was suspicious. May said they'd just started large-scale work here recently, and they were working in vampire territory. Were the dead vamps the ones who found out?

I glanced at my host. "How do you keep this hidden from the vampires?"

"Oh, we don't," she said. "We pay protection. Just like every business around here."

Well, there went that theory.

Eyes followed us as we walked through the room. I noticed that the workers didn't look very happy. "Is everyone here human?"

"Mostly. We have a few other species, but we have helped free many humans from their bonds to the vampires." She beamed with pride.

I looked at the faces of the people who were busy weighing and packing lotus. None of them looked like they were free. Despair practically filled the room like a cloud.

"This way," May said, taking us through a door.

We entered a hallway. Cement floors and steel walls. The temperature was warmer in here, like being inside a sauna. It made my senses prickle even more. There was so much wrong with this.

May opened another door, and we entered a makeshift office. A basic desk, several file cabinets, and metal folding chairs occupied the space. At least it was cooler in here.

"Babe?" May called. "You here?" She walked toward another door and it opened before she touched the door handle.

A familiar face appeared, and I wasn't fast enough at stifling my gasp. "Jimmy?"

His long hair was loose around his face, making him

look even more the viking I always saw him as. "What a surprise seeing you here, Isla."

"Wait, you two know each other?" May looked a little hurt.

"We go way back," Jimmy said.

May's jaw tensed, and she glared at me. It seemed she was having second thoughts about bringing me here.

"What is she doing here, May?" Jimmy asked without taking his eyes from me.

"I met her at Jack's. You said we didn't have anyone working the Crescent Pack. She's a human who lives there," May said.

"And he's a shifter who lives there," I said.

Now Jimmy was glaring at me.

"What?" May turned to Jimmy. "Tell me she's lying."

"I told you I was a shifter," he said. "You never asked about my pack."

"So you're dating him?" I asked.

"Obviously," she said.

"Did you even know what kind of shifter he was?" My brow furrowed. Growing up around shifters my whole life, I knew that pack was everything. It determined more about a shifter's personality than their own parents did. Each pack had expectations and standards. There were certain packs I'd never engage with.

"It didn't matter to me," she said.

She was so far out of her league. "You need to learn a little more about shifters and packs if you're going to get involved with one."

"I'm not involved. Dating someone doesn't make me involved," she said.

"You don't just date the shifter, you date their whole pack. How do you not know that?" I asked.

"This discussion is over. And Isla, you're leaving." Jimmy closed the door he'd just come through.

"You said the Crescent Pack was our only untapped territory," May said.

"We don't have anyone in the Crescent Pack for a reason," Jimmy said.

"You don't shit where you eat, huh, Jimmy?" I said.

"Don't pretend like you're perfect, Isla," he said. "Everyone knows you're fucking the vampire king."

"She's the one he's fooling around with?" May said. "Shit. Lily said she was kicked out for some scrawny human woman. Said he was all smitten and shit."

"I think you're getting wrong information," I said. "I wouldn't be stupid enough to get involved with a vampire."

"That's not true. Even Henry knows what you've been up to. He's letting it slide because he plans to use you," Jimmy said.

The words were far too close to the truth. My mind flashed to Henry's threats and words in the conference room.

I squeezed my hands into fists. Frustration curled in my belly. I wasn't fucking the vampire king. I mean, I had, but I didn't know who he was at the time and I hadn't since. Okay, also not fully true. But I stopped. I wasn't with him. And it had never been for information. I didn't use people like that.

"What the hell is going on here, Jimmy? Does Henry know about this?" I asked, gesturing toward the door I'd walked through.

"None of this is your business. And if you talk, I'll kill Maddie," Jimmy said.

"Listen, dude, I don't give a shit if you sell drugs. I'm just trying to figure out what the hell is going on here," I said.

"On who's orders? Henry's or the king's?" Jimmy asked.

I tensed.

"That's what I thought." Jimmy stepped toward me. "I've been telling Henry that you're more trouble than you're worth since the day he took you in. I knew buying you from your whore mom was a mistake. But he felt bad about killing your father."

"What?" The word came out breathless, and I felt like someone had just punched me in the gut.

My mom told me my dad had died in a motorcycle accident. That he'd been caught in a rainstorm and wiped out on a turn. Accidents were common enough that I never questioned it. Why would I? Who would lie about something like that?

Jimmy grinned, showing his teeth. His fangs weren't as elongated as a vampire, but wolf shifters had small fangs that gave them a far more predatory look than humans. "You didn't know you've been working for you daddy's murderer all these years."

I shook my head. "You're an asshole."

"I am, but I'm not lying about this," he said.

He was moving closer by the second and I could see the gold glint of his wolf flashing in his eyes.

I was in major trouble. My pulse kicked up and adrenaline surged. My mind seemed to scream, *run*.

Backing up slowly, I reached behind me for the door. As soon as I felt the doorknob, I turned, and I bolted from the room.

"Stop her!" Jimmy called.

Alarms blared, and all eyes were on me as I tore through the warehouse. Several huge guards moved in front of the door I'd entered through. I banked right, running toward a hallway that was unguarded.

One of them grabbed me and I went down, my chin smacking the cement floor so hard it blurred my vision. Pain shot through my skull and I held back the rising tears. I was not going down like this.

Kicking hard, my heel hit something and as soon as I heard the groan, I knew I'd struck where it hurt most. The hands on me vanished, and I scrambled to my feet only to have someone's arms close in around me from behind. I squirmed and grunted, kicking and bucking my hips in a failed attempt to free myself. Whoever was holding me was strong, and I wasn't moving.

"Let me go!" I shouted. "I'm no threat to you. I don't care if you want to sell drugs. Jimmy, let me go!"

Footsteps from behind, slow and deliberate. I tensed, waiting for the face of the shifter who'd never liked me to appear. Jimmy wore a deranged smile when he stopped in front of me. "I can't have you ruining years of planning. It's really not personal."

"It sure as fuck feels personal," I challenged.

Two other shifters joined us in the hallway, and my eyes widened in surprise. "Jack? Killian?" *Holy shit.* One of Derek's men and the beta himself. How high up the chain did this go? Was everyone in on it? Was the whole Crescent Pack selling lotus to humans beyond our city?

It would be the smartest move. Keep it out of our territory, and profit off the humans beyond our wards. It would be untraceable. How had I missed this?

"You're all in on this?" I felt so betrayed and so stupid.

"May really shouldn't have brought you here," Jimmy said.

I twisted again, trying to break free of the iron grip on me. "Please, just let me go."

"This isn't what I signed up for, Jimmy," Jack said. "I never agreed to this."

Jimmy growled, then charged toward the younger shifter. He grabbed a handful of his shirt and lifted him from the ground. Jack whimpered. "She's just a kid, man."

"Am I going to have a problem with you?" Jimmy said. "This whole thing falls apart if I don't have absolute loyalty."

"I'm loyal, you know that. But we don't murder humans. That's part of this," Jack pleaded.

"Jimmy," Killian's tone was a warning.

Jimmy glared at the beta, then lowered Jack to the ground. He smoothed his shirt, before looking right at him. "You're right. We don't murder humans." Then he grabbed Jack's head, and twisted fast. The cracking sound echoed through the hall and I might have screamed.

Killian charged Jimmy, knocking him to the ground. The other guards moved forward, unease in their steps. Killian punched Jimmy, and Jimmy attacked back. The grip around me didn't feel as secure as it was. My captor was distracted.

Taking a deep breath, I dropped to a crouch, slipping right through the slack grip. I didn't turn back to see if I was pursued. I just ran.

Not caring where I was headed as long as it was away from Jimmy, I sprinted forward, taking turns at random to try to throw my scent. With any luck, Killian would take him out and I could get away. At least all his guards were distracted. My throat tightened as the cost of the distraction hit me. Jack had stood up for me. He'd defended me. And he'd died as a result. I owed him my life.

I picked up my pace, a fresh wave of adrenaline coming from a dark thought. If I died, Jack's death was meaningless. I owed it to him to stay alive. I had to.

Spotting another door, I ran straight into it, pushing it open without concern for where it led. I emerged into a huge refrigerated room and skidded to a stop on the damp floor.

Sucking in a breath, my eyes widened in horror. My

whole body tensed, and I spun in a slow circle, taking in the death around me.

Dozens of bodies hung from huge metal meat hooks. Right through their chests. Heads lolling, skin blue-gray, eyes glassy, mouths agape, showing their fangs. Dark, bloody puddles stained the floor under the hanging bodies.

# CHAPTER
# TWENTY-SIX

Isla

MY STOMACH CHURNED, and my heart pounded. So many
dead vampires. A lump rose in my throat. There was no
way Jimmy was going to let me walk out of here now. Not
that I stood a chance before, drugs were one thing. Being
the vampire killer we were all hunting was so much worse.
It struck me how little I knew Jimmy. How could I know
him most of my life and not see the violent, deranged
streak of a serial killer lurking beneath? How had nobody
suspected him?

I knew I was running for my life, but it hadn't hit me
just how far he'd go. I had to get out of here.

Ahead, I saw another door and moved forward,
weaving between the bodies. I found myself peeking at the

faces, looking for Lucas. I didn't know if Anna had found him or if he was here among the dead.

The sound of a door opening and footsteps made my heart stop. I darted behind a hanging body. Bile rose in my throat, but I fought to keep myself grounded. I couldn't let this in. I couldn't let myself process the death and destruction until I was out of here.

Working to slow my breathing, I glanced for the door. I had to get out of here, but if I opened it, whoever was in here would know I was in here. Hiding was my only chance. I couldn't outrun a shifter.

My breath came out in clouds and time felt like it had stopped. Footsteps sounded on the cement floor. I didn't risk looking around the body to see if it was Jimmy or someone else.

"I can smell you in here." *Jimmy.* It was Jimmy. "And there's nobody here to save you."

He'd found me.

I raced for the door. I had to try. I had to find a way to survive. I was not going to die like this.

Massive, bloody hands slammed into the door just as I pulled it open. My whole body felt like it was vibrating with energy and fear. It was an intoxicating, overwhelming cocktail of emotions. I wasn't going to let him win. "Let me go, Jimmy."

"I should have killed you when you found that body at Marcus's," he said. "It was bad enough that I had to kill Marcus for being careless."

My breath hitched. "You were working with Marcus? You fucking hypocrite."

He grinned at me, his arms going to either side of me to cage me in. His mouth was covered in blood. His shirt was torn and his long hair was a tangled mess. He looked wild, and something dangerous glinted in his eyes. "I used him while he served his purpose. Once he was no longer useful, I got rid of him. Much like I'll do to you."

He leaned in closer. "I suppose I should thank you. You helped me speed up my timeline for getting rid of Killian and Jack."

"You're a monster," I said.

"No, the vampires are the real monsters. I'm just helping find a solution to their disease on this world," he said.

"I'm not part of this - whatever this is," I said. "Just let me go."

"So you can run off and tell your vampire boyfriend?" He scoffed. "Or Henry or the baby alpha? For a human, you sure got around."

I lifted a brow. Why was everyone so obsessed with my sex life? "You don't have any idea what you're talking about. None of them care what happens to me."

"That makes it easier for me. I won't have to cover up your death as carefully if nobody comes to look for you," he said.

I slipped down, though his arms and took off, heading for the other doors. He had a hold of me before I was even halfway across the room.

"You can't outrun me, little one," he said, tightening his grip around my arm.

I tugged, trying to get myself free. His fingers dug in and I winced against the pain.

We were in a section of the room where there weren't any bodies. There was no place for me to hide if I did get free. But there was something else I could use. Empty hooks swung from the ceiling. Their sharp points gleaming in the faint florescent light. The problem was getting it down so I could use it.

I took a deep breath, then let my shoulders sag. Slowly, I turned to face Jimmy. "Fine. I can't run from you. You've proven that. Cut me a deal instead," I suggested.

His brow furrowed. "What could I possibly want from you?"

"You said there's nobody selling in the Crescent Pack," I said. "I'm human. I've got status in the pack, unlike the other humans. They trust me. They'd buy from me. Or let me inform you about what's going on at the pack house. Henry trusts me. I can get close to him."

He laughed. "You'd sell your soul just like that?"

"I don't want to die," I said, working to keep my calm. I wasn't going to beg, but I needed him to lower his guard. His grip felt less intense, but I wasn't sure if it was because I was getting used to the pain or if he'd lightened up.

"I'm just a human. Does it matter who I work for?" I asked. "There isn't a whole lot for us here. Let me work in the warehouse if you don't want me to sell."

"The humans in the Crescent territories have their

ways of getting lotus. I don't need you," he said. "But if you could cozy up to Henry, you might be of use to me."

"He's interested in me," I said, hating myself. I refused to trade sex for information, but I needed out of here. Henry must not know about this, but once he found out, he was going to come for Jimmy. I just needed to get away from here. "I could help you. I could be loyal to you."

"Why would you defect from Henry? You've been inner circle since you were a kid. I don't know how you did it. No other human ever has, but you're not like other humans, are you?" He sneered.

"I was loyal, and look what it cost me. He offered me up to a vampire." I would play into his prejudice. Make him believe I could help him. "Henry lost my loyalty when he pawned me off on that bloodsucker."

Jimmy narrowed his eyes as if trying to determine if my words were true. Then he leaned in and smelled me. I tensed. Mother fucking shifters and their mother fucking obsession with scents.

"You smell like vampire," he hissed.

"Of course I do. He made me visit him," I reminded him.

"You also smell like something else. Something different," he said.

I shivered, the cold of the room getting to me. Or maybe it was from being too close to a psychopathic killer. Either way, I needed him to let me go. I needed out of here. "Jimmy, please. I can help you."

He growled and dropped my arm, and I let out a breath

of relief. It was going to be okay. I could get away from here and get help.

Suddenly, Jimmy's hand was around my throat. "You've always been a problem. A human too close to the wolves. And now you've cozied up to the vampires. You can't be trusted. You turn too easily."

"Like your girlfriend?" I hissed out between gasps.

"She serves her purpose," he said.

"And you judge me for my partners," I managed.

"You never knew when to shut the fuck up, did you?" He lifted me higher and my legs bicycled in the air as I tried to steady myself.

The world was getting fuzzy, and my vision blurred on the edges. But I was in the air, and I was so close to reaching one of those hooks.

"You're a coward." I spat in his face.

He roared, then lifted me a little higher, his fingers pressing harder against my windpipe. Thinking was nearly impossible as air ceased. With unsteady hands, I reached for the hook and lifted it off its track.

I swung, missing him completely. It was enough to throw him, though, and he released me from his grip. I landed hard on my knees, sucking in air while I shoved myself to standing.

Jimmy's eyes flashed gold, and his body began to break and shudder. He was going to change right here and tear me to shreds.

"I don't fucking think so." I lifted the hook and smashed it down on his back. He howled, twisting in agony. Half-wolf, half-man, he contorted toward me but I had already pulled the hook out and slammed it into him again.

This time, it impaled his side, and I pushed my foot into him, knocking him to the ground. I pulled the hook out and hit him again and again. The sharp end pounding into him. Blood sprayed and each time the hook landed it made a sickening sound, but I didn't stop. I hit him over and over until I was covered in blood and panting. My arms burned.

Finally, I realized he was fully dead. I dropped the hook on the cement and stared at the destroyed body. I'd bashed in his head and his body to the point where it was difficult to recognize him.

A new sensation spread through me as I realized what I'd done.

I was a monster.

I was no better than all those I feared.

What the fuck had I done?

Something deep inside me, as if calling from a place far away, told me to run. I had to get out of here. It was bad enough that I'd killed Jimmy. If I stayed, I was dead.

Somehow, my feet moved toward the door. It was like I was watching myself from outside my body. I didn't recognize the tangled emotions writhing within me. It was like a stranger was directing all my movements.

I was in a hallway. Alarm bells still blared. Lights flashed. But the hallway I was in was empty. Another door. It was locked, but somehow, I got it open. I didn't worry about how it happened, I just moved through in a daze.

I was in a loading dock, empty of people. Where were his guards? Why wasn't anyone blocking this? It didn't matter. Getting away from here was the only thing that mattered.

Running, I tore through the warehouses until I was back on the main road. At some point, my purse and phone had been lost. But it wasn't like I could call my roommate to come get me here, anyway. Technically, I wasn't even supposed to be here.

In vampire territory. Where I knew exactly one person.

Numb and covered in blood, I headed toward the king's mansion.

# CHAPTER
# TWENTY-SEVEN

Isla

THE SKY WAS inky purple with streaks of pale pink. The sun was low on the horizon. It would be dark soon. For now, the streets were mostly empty. Few vampires were old enough or powerful enough to walk in the sunlight.

The free pass through their territory wouldn't last long, though. I quickened my pace, my heart still pounding with adrenaline. All I could think of was the need to keep moving. I was determined to make it out of this in one piece.

A human in vampire territory covered in blood was like sending a whole pizza to a starving man. I knew how risky this was, but I didn't have any other choice. I'd never make it back to shifter territory on my own.

I also wasn't sure who I could trust.

Dante was hunting for the lotus dealers, and it didn't sound like he wanted to befriend them. Henry probably wasn't involved, but I couldn't be certain. Not when I'd seen Killian there. What if Henry was helping, but Jimmy was trying to take more than his share? I had no idea what Jimmy's plans were. All I knew was that he had killed so many vampires.

I shivered at the reminder of Jimmy. Of what I'd done to him. That was the biggest reason I couldn't go home. At least not right away. It was one thing to ask for forgiveness for sleeping with a vampire the alpha had practically pushed me toward. I had no idea what the consequence would be for killing a pack member.

It was self-defense, and it wasn't like it didn't happen from time to time. But I wasn't a shifter. I didn't have the same protection the wolves did.

I was nothing. I was like a pet. Jimmy was a respected member of the pack. He wasn't quite inner circle, but he was close. Henry trusted him. Compared to him, I was unimportant. Even if Jimmy saw me as something more, I never felt like I was. Henry always made a point of reminding me that I wasn't a wolf.

The ancient stone mansion was in view now. I hesitated, standing a block away. Was I making a huge mistake by trusting the vampire king? If I was, did I even have a choice?

This was it, my only option. Even if going home before

some other creature shredded me to ribbons or ate me for dinner, I had no idea what I'd be walking into at the Crescent Pack.

Forcing myself forward, I tried to think of what I'd say. How I'd explain what I'd seen. Dante would want to know about the dead vampires. He needed to know about Jimmy and the lotus. All of it. Nobody else should have to die for whatever twisted game Jimmy had been playing.

By the time I reached Dante's driveway, I was shaking and fear had replaced the aggression that had flowed through my veins. How had everything fallen apart so spectacularly?

Guards approached, and I held my hands in front of me where they could see them. "I'm unarmed."

"Stay back," one of them called. "Don't come any closer."

I stopped walking, looking toward the mansion at the end of that long driveway. Several lights flickered in the windows. Somehow, I knew he was home. He was awake, and he was there. I just needed him to see me.

"State your business," a guard called.

"I'm here to see the king," I said.

The guard looked at each other, then turned back to me. "The king doesn't see anyone without an appointment."

"He'll see me." Straightening my posture, I summoned all the confidence I could find. It wasn't real, but that didn't matter. I could pretend.

"He's not taking in new blood bags right now," one of the guards sneered.

I wasn't a blood bag. And it was the Dante's fault I was in this mess in the first place. If he'd never made me come give him answers, I wouldn't have even looked into the lotus trade. I'd still be sitting in my office filling out forms.

There was a very real possibility I was dead, anyway. How could anything possibly get any worse?

I was done being afraid.

Anger surged and my body tensed. "You will get him for me. Now."

"I don't know who you think you are," the guard sneered. "But you are going to turn around and go back to your hovel."

Both guards moved forward, then suddenly tripped and landed on their faces.

I took a step back at the sudden movement and the sound of their bodies hitting the ground.

"What the hell?" one of them cried out. Vines were wrapped around their feet and ankles. "Where did this come from?"

Both guards pulled at the vines, but they grew back every time they snapped them. The vegetation climbed them like a snake, slithering around their legs, wrapping and tightening.

They started to scream.

I ran toward the mansion, leaving them with whatever strange magic had halted them from attacking me.

The front door opened and a rectangle of light glowed like a beacon in the rapidly growing darkness. A figure filled the light, and I knew it was Dante.

He was at my side in a heartbeat, his hands gripping my upper arms. "Where are you hurt?"

"It's not my blood," I said.

His large hand cupped the side of my face, and I leaned into his touch. "Tell me who did this to you."

"I told you, it's not my blood."

"Your pulse is racing and I can smell the fear. I don't care if you won the battle; nobody should have touched you," he said. "Tell. Me. Who. Did. This."

"It was Jimmy, a shifter from the Crescent Pack. He's dead now. But, Dante..."

His eyes widened just a little, and something about his expression softened. "You used my name."

Had I never said it out loud before? "Don't change the subject." I said. "There's more."

"Stop, trespasser!" a voice called.

I turned to see the two guards, finally free of their vines, racing forward.

Dante pushed me behind him, blocking me from them. "What is the meaning of this?"

"She used magic, tied us up with vines," one of them said.

"I did no such thing," I spat. "I told you I needed to see him."

"We tried to stop her," the other said.

Dante walked over to them, his movements slow and purposeful. Both guards tensed but waited. Neither spoke.

The king stopped in front of them. Then his movements were like lightning. He grabbed the first guard's head and turned it fast. The cracking sound sliced through the quiet night air. The second guard didn't even have time to react before his head was turned to the side, the second crack making me shiver.

Both bodies hit the ground with a thud.

It was the same thing Jimmy had done to Jack. My lower lip quivered. Maybe I'd made a mistake coming here.

Dante turned to me. "I'm sorry for their behavior."

"You didn't need to kill them," I said.

"They'll wake in a few hours," he said. "But they won't deny you again."

I blew out a relieved breath I didn't know I'd been holding. It wasn't quite the same as Jimmy. How fucked up was my life that I was feeling gratitude for Dante's actions? I really needed to get away from these supernaturals. There was no way this was what life was like in human cities.

"Come inside. Let me help you get cleaned up and you can tell me everything." Dante extended his hand.

I didn't even flinch when I took it.

After everything I'd been through in the last few weeks, the only presence in my life who hadn't harmed me was the vampire king. It didn't excuse what he'd involved me in, or his seduction when he knew damn well that I was part of the Crescent Pack, but right now, I couldn't bring myself to care about any of that.

He radiated safety.

I knew I was beyond fucked up to feel safe with him. I'd watched him kill. I knew what he was capable of. I was like a bug to him. He could squish me without effort.

Yet, I followed him to a large bathroom and watched as he filled an oversized clawfoot tub.

When he helped me undress, I didn't fight him. I stood in front of him, naked and bloody. I didn't even care that he was taking in every inch of my bare skin.

His hands didn't wander as he guided me into the warm water. I hissed as it came into contact with injuries I didn't remember receiving.

As he gently washed the blood off my face and shoulders, I winced when the cloth grazed my bruised neck. Dante stopped, the cloth inches from my skin. "Jimmy did this to you?"

I nodded.

He carefully returned to cleaning me off, then he stood. "I'm going to send in someone to help you wash your hair."

"Dante, you should know I was at a warehouse. Here. In vampire territory. Number twenty-seven, I think. There was lotus. So much lotus."

"I will never regret anything more than I do at getting you involved in this," he said.

My brow furrowed. Those weren't the words I

expected from the cocky vampire king who was using a human to get information he couldn't.

"There's more," I said.

He waited patiently.

"There were vampires. A lot of them. All hanging in a refrigerated room. Just like the others," I said. "I think Jimmy was the one killing the vampires."

"Please, please don't leave. I'm going to send in Anna. I'll be back soon." He left the bathroom before I could object.

I sunk under the warm water until my lungs cried out for air. When I emerged, I carefully scrubbed my face, still feeling blood that might or might not even be there. I wasn't sure I was ever going to shake the feeling of Jimmy's blood on me.

My head ached, my chin hurt, everything hurt. It was going to take a while to recover from this.

"You're still alive," Anna said as she walked into the bathroom.

"I'm lucky," I said.

"Yes, you are," she said. "It's been a while since I acted as a lady in waiting, but I'm hoping that skills don't atrophy."

I smiled, then winced. Even smiling hurt. "You don't need to be here. I can take care of myself."

"Oh, I have no doubts about that anymore. You killed a wolf shifter," she said. "That's impressive."

My shoulders tensed, and my stomach twisted. I was a

murderer. Jimmy was going to kill me, but I didn't want to take his life.

"You did the right thing," she said.

The scent of jasmine filled the air and Anna's hands lathered the floral soap into my hair. I let my eyes flutter closed as she massaged my scalp with expert precision.

I knew I should feel weird right now. I was letting a strange vampire woman wash my hair. I was naked in a tub inside the vampire king's house. There was nothing normal about this.

But I was tired to my bones. An exhaustion that left me unable to respond to the little thoughts telling me to question what was happening.

Unless I was in danger, I wasn't sure I was in any position to argue anything at the moment.

It was an odd sort of numbness or acceptance. I wasn't sure which. Either way, I let Anna wash my hair and help me into a white, fluffy robe.

"Can I get you anything?" she asked after she finished brushing and braiding my hair.

I had to admit, by the time she was finished, I felt like a fucking queen. "No, I'm fine."

"How about some tea?" she asked. "The first kill is the hardest."

I caught her eyes in the reflection of the mirror and the two of us stared at each other for a long while. "I didn't want to kill him."

"Most of us don't kill because we want to. We kill because we need to survive." She squeezed my shoulder.

My throat was tight, and I wasn't sure I could speak without tears breaking free, so I stayed quiet.

"I'll get you some tea. Wait here. It's not safe out there for you after dark," she said. "In this house, you are safe. You have my word."

After she walked out of the bathroom, I broke down. The tears didn't stop for a long while.

# CHAPTER
# TWENTY-EIGHT

Isla

A POT of tea and an empty cup sat on a small table nestled between a pair of chairs in the bedroom. I hadn't even looked around when I'd walked through with Dante. It was a large master suite. A king-size canopy bed with thick, heavy curtains tied off on the posts protruded from the center of the back wall. A large fireplace faced the bed and a large wood wardrobe was pushed up against the side wall. Next to the sitting area where the tea waited was a pair of double doors leading to a balcony.

I bypassed the tea and walked right to the balcony, craving some fresh air. I wasn't stupid enough to flee from the mansion right into vampire territory. Not at night, at least. During the day would be a risk, but nowhere near the risk level of trying to make my way through in the dark.

The doors swung in, and I stepped out into the crisp night air. It was still pretty warm, despite the fact that the sun was completely gone. The moon was a sliver of silver among a dusting of stars.

I inched forward and caught sight of a sprawling garden below. I took a deep breath, closing my eyes as I reveled in the scents of the night-blooming flowers. Leave it to a vampire to have a garden mostly consisting of evening blooms. It made me smile and made me feel a little safer here. It was almost like my grandmother was looking out for me.

"Isla?" Anna's voice was barely above a whisper.

I turned to where she was standing in the middle of the room.

"You alright?"

"No," I said.

"Yeah, I didn't think so," she said. "You will be. But give yourself some time."

"You're close to him, aren't you?" Anna was the one who'd come to ask about the flowers, and who Dante had sent to help me tonight. But I knew she was capable of far more. I could almost feel the power coiled within her.

"I'm not his lover, if that's what you're asking," she said.

"It's not," I said entirely too quickly.

She smirked like a cat who'd cornered a mouse. That predatory gleam always present in her expression.

I shivered, overly aware of the fact that I was alone in a room with an incredibly powerful vampire. Like Dante, she could walk in the day without any sign of discomfort.

"I won't harm you," she said. "Even if I wanted to, Dante made it clear to everyone what would happen if anyone touched you."

My brow furrowed. "And what's that?"

She made an amused sound. "You have no idea, do you?"

"Consider me out of the loop on everything," I said.

Anna's eyes looked me up and down before settling back on my face. "I suppose you wouldn't."

I sighed. "Whatever. I don't have time for supernatural drama."

"The drama is just getting started," she said.

"We got the bad guy," I said. "I just need to figure out how I'm going to explain this to my boss so I can go home."

"You still want to go home after all this?" she asked.

"It's only temporary." I wasn't sure why I said it, but the words tumbled out. "I'm leaving Lost Harbor."

She blinked, and I think I actually surprised her. "When?"

"On the new moon, after the summer solstice," I said.

"That soon?"

"I haven't told anyone that yet," I said. "I'm not sure why I told you."

"Then it's not my secret to share," she said.

"You won't tell him?" I wasn't sure why I cared. What

did it matter if Dante found out I was leaving? It wasn't like we owed each other anything.

"I won't," she said. "But just so you know, I haven't kept a secret from him in centuries. It's going to cost you."

My heart picked up speed. "Oh?"

"A favor, at another time," she said.

Favors were currency in our world. We learned from a young age that you never wanted to be in debt to anyone. The fae were the worst, of course, but it wasn't ideal to be indebted to any creature.

Knowing that, I still found myself nodding in agreement. For some reason, I really didn't want him to know I was leaving soon.

Anna smiled, her fangs glinting in the dim light.

I really hoped I didn't regret this agreement. Part of me wanted to take it back, but before I could open my mouth, an explosion shattered the sounds of the night. Car alarms blared and my pulse raced.

We both ran to the balcony just as a second explosion ripped through the air. Flames appeared, sparks flew, and smoke curled into the inky sky.

My blood ran cold.

"That's the warehouse district," I said.

"I'd say you don't have to worry about your pack finding out what you did," Anna said.

"Dante did that?" My hands trembled. All those people inside the warehouse. All those humans.

"I told you, he made it clear that nobody was to touch you," she said.

"Why?" I wasn't sure if I wanted to know why he destroyed it or why he cared what happened to me. Maybe both.

"He protects what's his," she said.

"I'm not his." How many times was I going to have to say it?

"You have been since the moment he set his eyes on you," she said.

A chill ran down my spine, but I don't think it had anything to do with her words. There was a presence behind me. Something calling to me, urging me to respond.

I turned slowly, my stomach in knots as anticipation swirled. I already knew what I'd see. None of it made sense, but I was still too overwhelmed to allow myself to process anything.

Once I opened myself up to question one thing, everything was going to flood in. I'd have to face the full weight of what I'd done.

I wasn't ready for that.

My breath left my lungs when I came face to face with the vampire king. He wasn't hiding any inch of the monster that lurked beneath.

Eyes blazing, fangs extended, body tense, hands and face covered in blood. He was everything we'd been warned about.

And I didn't feel a single flicker of fear. Not one. My heart stuttered, and I stepped toward him. "Are you hurt?"

The curve of his lips was animalistic and self-assured.

The liquid silver of his eyes stilled, calming like a sea after a storm. "It's not my blood."

I bit down on my lower lip to keep from smiling. I should be concerned, but hearing him use the same response I'd given him sent a shock of something dark and twisted into me. I was happy to see him.

Something was very wrong with me.

His hand reached for me, gently brushing across my neck. "Does it hurt?"

I touched my throat. "It's not too bad."

He lowered his hand. "None of them can hurt you again."

My breath hitched. "The humans?"

"I knew you'd ask me about them," he said.

My brows lifted in silent question.

"I killed all the guards," he said. "Anyone who might have hurt you."

"The workers?" I asked.

"I let them run before I blew it up," he said.

Into vampire territory, where they'd likely become someone's next meal. At least they had a chance.

"I've never shown mercy like that before." He closed the distance between us. "What have you done to me?"

"You don't even know me," I said. "We've barely even spoken."

His crimson coated hands were on my face, gently coaxing my chin up so I could stare into his silver eyes. Blood coated his face and neck, but his fangs had retracted, giving his mouth a human quality that could easily lure someone into a sense of false security.

Was that what was happening? Was I falling into some kind of trick? "Did you compel me?"

He gently shook his head. "Never."

It would have explained the draw to him. Part of me wanted it to be magic that created the pull I felt. But I knew it wasn't compulsion. I could feel the truth in his words, see it in the way he studied my face.

A million reasons to walk away raced through my mind, but none of them lingered. I was leaving soon, but there was no way this was more than a conquest. He wanted me because I'd turned him down. If I caved, if I gave him what he wanted, maybe he'd let me go.

The thought made my chest tighten. I wasn't sure I wanted either of us to walk away. But that was insane. There could never be anything besides sex between us.

His bloody hand toyed with the end of my braid. I could almost feel the heat between us. I didn't have supernatural senses, but it didn't take them to know what we both wanted.

I'd nearly died. Everything in my life was falling apart. I deserved this. I deserved to feel safe and alive.

I didn't even care that he was covered in blood as I rose to my toes and pressed my lips against his.

# TWENTY-NINE

Isla

He grabbed a fistful of my hair and yanked my head back, his mouth devouring mine. He tasted like blood and sin and everything dark and delicious. Everything I wasn't supposed to have but desperately needed. His tongue brushed against my teeth and my lips parted, allowing him to slide into my mouth. Our tongues met in a frenzy of heat and passion. I couldn't get enough of him.

I could feel the points of his fangs, the reminder of exactly what he was and exactly what he could do to me. He was forbidden on every level, but I didn't care. I was done resisting him.

The kiss was like fire, sending heat rushing through me. Each movement of his lips, the stroke of his tongue, gained in intensity until I was gasping for breath.

My fingers tangled into his dark hair, and I pulled him closer to me, desperate to feel every inch of his body against mine. His hands moved lower, caressing and exploring until his fingers reached the belt of the robe, freeing the knot. A rush of air greeted my bare skin as the robe dropped to the ground and I came alive under the feel of his rough hands on my flesh.

Everywhere he touched left a trail of red, the remains of the dead guards he'd killed for me. All of them gone because of the harm they'd caused me. Goosebumps erupted across my skin and I sucked in a breath, pulling away from the kiss.

He made me feel safe. He made me feel alive.

I wasn't sure I'd ever felt like that before.

I studied him, the blood and fangs; the swirling silver depths of his eyes. We were both panting, the heat between us undeniable. There was a pull, something deeper and more intense than anything I'd ever experienced.

He brought me to life. After melting into the background and living for a future that was simply a hope that things might get better.

This was what I was missing. This spark I felt. I never wanted to let it go.

I grinned, then leaped onto him, wrapping my bare legs around his waist. He growled, his hands going around my ass to hold me against him. Our lips crashed together; the kiss was so desperate and intense my lips hurt. I pressed harder. Taking the pain with the pleasure.

Gently, he lowered me to the bed and removed his mouth from mine. Covered in blood, fangs were extended, he stared at me with those molten silver eyes.

I'd never wanted him more.

He was on full display for me. Not hiding any part of himself. This was him. This was Dante. He was brutal and vicious. He killed and fed and fucked. I didn't know why I wasn't running from him or why seeing him this way made me even hungrier for him.

I needed him.

Dante seemed to hesitate, staring down at me with a look of admiration that reminded me of the way Kaylie and Maddie looked at each other. It felt so real. As if this wasn't just about sex.

That little flicker of fear, the part of me that avoided intimacy and connection, flared to life. This wasn't just sex, and I knew it. I couldn't pretend it meant nothing the way I had when we'd been together in the past. If I did this, it meant something.

My chest tightened, and my heart raced. I didn't want to stop him. I didn't care what it meant. I'd deal with my feelings later. "Why did you stop?"

He leaned over me and pressed his palm to the side of my face. "If we keep going, I'm not going to stop. I won't go easy on you, Love."

"Haven't you given me enough warnings now to know that I'm not going to listen to you?" I teased.

He smirked. "You are so wicked."

I sat up and crawled across the bed to where he was

standing. "You're still wearing clothes." I worked the button of his jeans and he removed his shirt. I took in every inch of him. His chest, neck, and arms were covered in tattoos. I dragged my fingers down his torso, lingering on a tattoo of a trio of roses. I was certain every tattoo had a meaning, but that could wait for another time. I climbed off the bed and pushed him to the edge of the mattress.

He arched a brow, but I just smirked. "Your turn to sit."

His tongue swiped across his lower lip slowly as his gaze dipped to my naked body. I used his distraction to push him again. He sat on the bed, then reached for me. I moved just far enough away that he couldn't grab me. "Naughty, king."

He chuckled. "You know, it's never a good idea to tease a vampire."

I dropped to my knees in front of him and set my hands on his thighs. "My turn to see how you taste."

I dragged my tongue from the base of his cock up to the tip, circling around the head before closing my lips around him fully. He groaned, then fisted my hair, guiding my head as I bobbed and licked. His hips bucked, and I struggled to take all of him. I continued until I had as much of him in my mouth as I could, adding my hand to the base. He sucked in a sharp breath, reacting to my movements. I enjoyed the thrill of knowing that I was in control. His cock twitched, and I picked up the pace, thinking he might be close.

Suddenly, he shoved me off and grabbed my chin with his hand, guiding me to standing. "You are such a good little cocksucker, Love. But I'm not ready to be done with you."

He was on his feet, and then I was tossed on the bed. He was on top of me in an instant, roughly spreading my legs apart. He grabbed my thighs and pulled me toward him.

"My turn," he said as he lowered himself to my center. His tongue moved over the bundle of nerves, making me gasp. He started slowly, making lazy circles with his tongue. My breath hitched and tension built low in my belly. Then the swirls changed to more intense movements. His tongue flicked quickly, making my hips rise and my back arch as the pleasure built.

I was nearly there, close to reaching climax, when his fingers dipped inside, curling just right. I shattered, crying out as the orgasm sent shivers through me. He didn't stop. His fingers continued to thrust, his tongue and lips worked against my clit. The pressure built again, quicker this time, until my hips were bucking and I was screaming as a series of climaxes rolled through me like waves; one after the other, building off one another until I was panting and begging for a break.

Dante lifted his face, his mouth still bloody, but now covered with a sheen of glossy liquid from my pussy. He licked each of his fingers, getting the blood along with my juices. My heart was racing, my breaths came out in rapid pants.

"You're delicious," he said.

"You can taste me for real if you want," I said, unsure

why I was offering. I'd never thought I'd let a vampire feed from me, but I wanted him to. I wanted to feel that with him, and I wanted to give myself to him fully.

"You'd let me feed from you?" He looked surprised.

I nodded. The weight of what I'd offered made my throat feel thick. There were people who offered their blood freely, but I had no doubt Dante knew what this meant to me. It was a connection that I didn't even know I wanted.

"You don't know what you're asking, Love," he said.

"I do," I said.

He grinned, then settled his hips between my thighs. He leaned down, then pressed a kiss to my jaw before moving to my neck. My breath hitched and for a moment, I thought he would bite me.

Instead, he kissed my neck before letting those fangs scrape gently across the sensitive skin. His lips moved to my ear. "One day, I will feed from you. But not tonight. Not after everything you've been through."

I was a little hurt, but before I could process what I was feeling, his cock slid into my opening. My hips rose to meet him and I gasped as I adjusted to him inside me.

He grabbed my thighs, pulling my hips up until they were elevated above the bed. He pounded into me, hard and fast. I gripped the sheets, gasping for breath as each thrust took me closer to the edge. Pressure built, and I leaned into the feeling, letting the orgasm split through me.

Dropping my thighs, he leaned over me, our bodies

close. I wrapped my arms around him, my eyes finding his. Those silver depths still called to me, urging me to fall into them. I dug my fingernails into his back and he lowered his face until our lips met. He kissed me as if it was our first and last kiss, the intensity sending me over the edge again. He groaned into my mouth as he found his release, then he pulled back from the kiss, nipping at my lower lip with his teeth.

I bit back, and he hissed out a breath. "You really are wicked."

Satisfied and sleepy, we curled up together on the bed. My head rested in the crook of his shoulder and for the first time in a long time, I felt content to just be. There was no pressure to get things done or make plans. I could simply exist.

# CHAPTER
# THIRTY

Isla

"You have a visitor," Dante said, easing up to sitting.

I sat with him, my hand still intertwined in his. I was already missing the feel of his arm around me. "What do you mean?"

"There's a shifter at my door," he said.

"You can sense that from here?" I asked.

He smirked. "No. Anna told me."

"So you two can see in each other's heads?" The expression on my face must have given away my concern. I wasn't sure I liked the idea of someone else watching through his eyes.

He laughed, the sound surprisingly soft and playful. I didn't know he was capable of such a sound. "We can send messages, communicate. Don't worry. Everything between us is private."

"Can she read thoughts?" I remembered about the feeling I got from her when she'd been outside my office. The roses and the note felt like so long ago. How did we end up here, tangled in his sheets, after all that?

"She's had centuries to learn to read expressions and body language. She's rarely wrong," he said.

"What about you?" I asked.

He opened his mouth, then closed it. "We'll talk more about me later. Right now, I think you better go calm down your alpha."

"Not my alpha," I said through gritted teeth.

"That's not how he sees it," Dante warned.

With a heavy sigh, I peeled myself away from him, already missing the intimacy of his touch. Something was very, very wrong with me. Was I so starved for affection that I was willing to risk everything for a tumble with a vampire? It seemed like the only option when he'd returned from destroying the warehouse. I had needed it as much as him.

As I wrapped the robe around me, I couldn't find even an ounce of regret. I wanted Dante. Still wanted him.

The vampire appeared in front of me, a washcloth in hand. "I got some blood on you."

"Oh, yeah." He was still covered in the blood of those dead guards, and I hadn't even cared. It was like I was someone different around him. Someone who didn't over-think everything. With Dante, I let myself feel. Be. Exist.

With him, I was fully present rather than just going through the motions.

I wasn't sure if I'd ever let myself open up to my emotions and senses this much. It made me feel more alive than I had in years.

My heart kicked against my ribs as I watched his focused expression. His touch was gentle as he wiped the blood from my face, my neck, my collarbones. Then he took my hands and wiped each clean.

When he was done, he stared at me for a moment, as if he was lost in thought. I didn't feel uncomfortable under his gaze. Instead, I stared back, memorizing every inch of him.

He lifted my hand to his lips and pressed a soft kiss on the back of my palm. "All better."

I swallowed hard. "Thank you."

"You should go talk to Henry before he pisses off Anna," he said.

"I might want to see that," I said.

"Anna is less patient than I am," he warned. "She wouldn't let him off with a warning."

"Understood." I headed back downstairs.

Henry sucked in a breath when he saw me, then he gave Anna a nasty glare before storming forward. "Where have you been?"

"Doing what you asked me to do," I snapped.

"I didn't think you'd actually fuck the blood bag," he said.

"Isn't that what you wanted me to do?" I asked with mock innocence.

"If this is your idea of a joke..."

"It's not a joke, Henry. One of your people tried to kill her. She's lucky she's not dead." Dante's voice was smooth and radiated authority.

"What are you talking about?" Henry demanded.

"I followed a lead and found Jimmy running a lotus operation," I said.

Henry's brow furrowed. "Jimmy? Lotus?"

"That's not all," I added quickly. "I found a ton of dead vampires. It was Jimmy. He was killing them."

"I don't understand. He was running lotus? Why kill vampires?" Henry asked.

"I don't know," I said. "Did you know?"

"No. I might not like vampires, but I'd never condone a serial killer. I'm not sick," he said.

"Not that, the lotus," I said, thinking of my mom. I wasn't convinced it would have no lasting impact on her. Everything had a price.

Henry shook his head. "No. A few months ago, someone came to me asking to run lotus through our pack. I declined. It might not be as lethal for us as it is for your kind," he lifted his chin toward Dante, "but it's still deadly to most supernaturals. I don't want that shit around."

"And here I thought you didn't have any moral limits," I said.

"Watch it, Isla," Henry warned. "Just because you helped with this doesn't mean you can talk back."

Dante growled.

Henry smirked. "You can growl at me all you want, but she's not your concern. Whatever she did with you, it was because I told her to. I told her to get the information from you."

Dante's brow furrowed the slightest bit, and he looked at me. I swear I could feel his heart breaking.

"That's not true and you know it," I snapped.

"So this is what - love?" Henry laughed. "She played you, *your highness*. Because I own her and she answers to me. I told her to fuck you. She followed orders."

I shook my head. "No, that's not what happened."

"Speak your next words very carefully," Dante said.

"She hates all of us. Your kind as much as mine," Henry said. "She's just human, after all."

"I don't hate anyone," I said.

"Oh? You're denying that you paid a smuggler to get you out of town after the solstice?" Henry asked.

I froze.

"You think I don't know everything that happens in my pack?" He scoffed, then looked at Dante. "She broke off her engagement with the future alpha and booked passage out of town. You think she gives a shit about you? She must be damn good to fool someone your age."

"You don't know what you're talking about," I said.

"Are you leaving Lost Harbor?" Dante asked. "Did you book passage with a smuggler?"

My throat felt tight. It had been my plan for so long. There had never been any reason to stay. For the first time since my grandmother's death, I wondered if there was something here worth staying for. Being with Dante made me feel alive. "I set it up a year ago."

"You should go," he said.

"Women, am I right?" Henry laughed.

I glared at him. "I didn't do this for you."

"Whatever helps you sleep at night, sweetheart," Henry said.

"Anna, see that Isla gets home safely," Dante said.

"Dante..." I turned to the king, but he was already walking away.

"Come on, Isla, I'll drive you home," Anna said.

Henry's fingers closed around my upper arm. "I'll take her from here. The killer is dead. There's no reason for her to be involved anymore. I need my accountant back."

I glanced back one last time, but Dante wasn't even in sight.

"Come on, Isla. You're lucky we're going now before he uses his magic to make you fall even harder." Henry tugged on my arm.

I looked at Anna, my expression pleading. Silently asking her if that was what happened. Dante had denied any compulsion, and I'd believed him.

Anna looked down, not meeting my gaze. "You should go."

A painful lump filled my throat, and I clenched my jaw, working to keep my expression as blank as possible. I didn't want her to see how much pain I was in. I'd fallen right into the seduction. Over and over. Unable to deny him, even when I knew it would put my life at risk. What other explanation was there besides magic?

I turned away from Anna and let Henry lead me through the open front door.

We were silent until Henry pulled into the parking lot in front of my apartment. "You did good, kid."

I looked over at him. "Did you know Jimmy was the type?"

He shook his head. "He hid it well. I'd only ever seen him go after his enemies. Sometimes I sent him to do things. But I didn't think he enjoyed it. I didn't think he'd go after vampires or anyone else like that."

"What about the lotus?" I asked.

"We'll figure it out," he said. "But not tonight. You've been through enough."

Henry had never been this understanding before. My brow furrowed. "Why are you being so nice?"

"You're the best at what you do," he said.

"Even if I leave?" I asked.

"I'm not going to stop you. Mostly because it'll help Ryder get over you," he said.

"When did you find out?"

"Remember when I replaced you with Gina?" He glanced over at me.

"That makes sense," I said.

"I want something in return, though," he said.

Here it comes. I sucked in a breath and raised my brows, waiting for the other shoe to drop.

"Can you please help train her? She's the best we've got, and she's terrible. You don't leave for a while. Maybe you can show her the ropes."

It was the last thing I expected. I thought he'd try to stop me but I supposed getting rid of me benefitted him since Ryder couldn't shake his feelings for me. "Just so you know, Ashley would literally do anything to be on Ryder's arm."

"I know," he said. "He won't give anyone the time of day while you're here."

"I didn't mean to hurt him," I said. "I swear I've been nothing but honest with him. I'm not right for him."

"I know," Henry said. "Now, get out of here. We've got a big mess to clean up, and I want you at work bright and early tomorrow morning."

"You got it, boss," I said as I opened the door.

What a weird fucking day.

Maddie launched to her feet the second she saw me. "Why do you smell like blood?"

I shook my head. I was not going to miss the shifter senses when I left. My insides twisted. Maddie didn't know. Everyone was going to know soon.

"Sit, please. I have so much to tell you." I explained everything. What happened in the warehouse, what I'd done with Dante, even my plans to leave. My heart ached as I glossed over my time with Dante. The memory of him.

At the end of the conversation, Maddie's eyes welled

with tears. "I always knew this day would come." She stood and left the room.

I stayed on the couch, confused and wondering if I should follow her. Before I could decide, she was on her way back in, carrying a shoe box.

She set it on the table, then took the top off. It was full of cash.

"What is this?" I asked.

"I stashed a few dollars every week since we moved in here in case you ever needed to bail," she said. "Being human in this city is not easy."

"You've been saving this that long?" Now I was in tears. "I can't accept this."

"You can and you will," she said. "And it's not forever. I can leave and visit. It's you who has been trapped here."

I pulled her into a hug. For some reason, having her support made this feel harder. I'd blocked out all the good in Lost Harbor, worried it would make me stay. But it left me feeling empty and numb. In the last few days, I remembered what it was like to be alive. And as I expected, those thoughts made me wonder if leaving was the right choice.

# CHAPTER
# THIRTY-ONE

DANTE

"THE SHIFTERS ARE GOING to think everything is tied up in a nice little bow," Anna said as she strolled into the screened in patio.

"That's good. We don't need them poking around," I said.

"What happens when more vampires die?" she asked.

"They might not. I do think we got the guy who was draining them and leaving them to rot," I said.

"Torn to pieces and scattered is more his style," Anna said.

"When he does the dirty work himself," I agreed. "We have no way of knowing if he's got more goons around that he's recruited."

She stood in front of me for a moment in silence. It

was a lot to take in. We'd been through this before. Bodies, both human and vampire, and a trail of lotus. Each time we got closer, things fell apart. But this felt different. This operation wasn't meant to be temporary. It felt like it was constructed to be his new home base. Which was ironic when you considered that Lost Harbor was where he gained eternal life in the first place.

"You're just going to let her walk away?" Anna asked.

I looked at my friend and shook the thoughts of my brother away. "You mean Isla?" Even saying her name was painful.

"Yes, her," she said. "You're really not going to see her again?"

"It's what I should have done from the beginning," I said.

"She was tied up and naked. You can't tell me you wish you'd have left her there," Anna snapped.

"Of course not, but after that. I should have left the party, left her alone," I said. "If Vincent found her, I'd never forgive myself. She's safer if she leaves."

"Everyone deserves a chance at happiness, Dante. Even you," Anna said.

"No, not everyone." I had too much blood on my hands. I knew what I was. What I'd done. Isla was a sick joke. The universe handing me the perfect woman and making her human, vulnerable, and absolutely unattainable.

I should be grateful I even got the time with her that I had. I didn't even deserve that.

"She's not leaving yet." Anna sat on the armrest of the couch, turning toward me. "There's no reason you can't be with her for a short time. That's all mortals have, anyway."

"You know exactly why I can't do that. If she finds out, she might stay. I can't take that choice from her. She wants out of this hellhole and I don't blame her," I said.

"See how much you have in common? You both hate Lost Harbor," Anna said.

"Yeah, but she hates it because of what me and my family did to it. I hate it for another reason," I said darkly.

"No. Same reason. Your family is to blame for all of it," she said.

I raised my brows. She had a point. *Vincent.* He was the cause of so much pain for so many. He was like a plague.

When I'd destroyed the warehouse, I knew what I was doing. It was the largest operation we'd found. There was no way it wouldn't be on his radar. All this time chasing him and we might have finally flushed him out.

"He's probably already on his way here," Anna said.

I looked up at her. "I hate it when you do that."

She smirked. "Then don't make yourself so fucking easy to read."

"Another reason to keep my distance," I said. "But I want someone to watch her. Make sure she's safe till she gets out of here or until we get rid of Vincent."

Anna nodded. "I have someone in mind."

"Good."

She laughed softly and my brow furrowed. "What's so funny?"

"After all these years of chasing him, I never thought the final showdown would be here. Back where we started," she said. "Fucking Lost Harbor."

I blew out a breath. "Yeah. Maybe we should burn the whole place to the ground and be done with it."

"It might come to that when we finally face him," Anna said.

I stood, feeling restless and angry. So much wasted time spent hunting him down. All these years and it brings me back here. To the one place I didn't want to be.

And it brought me to Isla.

Fate was so fucking cruel.

"How about I watch over her?" Anna said softly.

I shook my head and smiled. I really was an open book tonight. "That would help." I could use her with the Vincent problem, but I knew I wasn't going to focus if I was worried about Isla.

"I'll go now," she said. "Make sure she's home safe."

"Thank you," I said. "You know, I might be wrong about her."

Anna paused in the doorway. "You could be, but I doubt it. Wouldn't be the first case of a vampire forming a bond with a human."

"I'm not entirely sure she's human," I confessed.

Her brow furrowed. "What do you mean?"

"There was an incident. Magic used on the guards when she arrived," I said.

"How did she hide that from you?" Anna asked.

"I don't think she knows. And I'm not going to tell her," I said. "She wants to leave, and I don't have any right to ruin her plans. Especially when it'll put her life at risk."

"What if she wanted you to ask her to stay?" Anna pressed.

"You heard that wolf. He told her to bed me." I let out a growl of frustration. "Why the fuck would the fates stick me with a mating bond at a time like this, anyway?"

She shrugged. "I don't make the rules. If I did, I'd have forged a bond between myself and a nice guy and been done with all this."

"You'd never leave me," I said.

"Oh, there's the cocky asshole I know and love." She winked, then left me alone with my thoughts.

I sat back down and ran a hand through my hair. I'd give myself tonight to mourn what I'd lost. What I'd given up. But tomorrow, I couldn't dwell. There was too much to do. I had to let her go. She probably didn't feel the bond anyway and by letting her live her life, I was giving her more than she could ever have with me.

*Dante.* Anna's voice rang in my head. Full of fear and panic.

I ran to where she was standing by the front door, taking in her terrified expression before looking down to see the severed head.

*Shit.* Luke's dead eyes stared up at us. I balled my hands into fists and my nostrils flared as anger surged.

"Fuck," Anna said. "When you didn't find him at the warehouse, I really thought maybe he skipped town."

I had hoped for the same thing. It wouldn't have been the first time he took a few days to clear his head. He never warned us when he did, but he always came back ready and focused.

Luke had a hard life. He'd seen too much and lived through too much pain. I gave him space when he needed it because he always had my back. "I failed him."

Anna kneeled and removed something that was stuck in Luke's hair. "You didn't fail him. This was personal."

She handed me a piece of paper written in an ancient, dated script that could only belong to one person.

*The age of vampires is over. I'm coming for all of you.*

I crumpled the paper and threw it as hard as I could.

"Well, I guess that answers that question," Anna said.

"Yeah. Vincent is already here," I said.

---

THANK YOU FOR READING *OBSESSION*. Look for book 2, *Hunger,* later this summer. The pre-order will be available on Amazon soon!

# About the Author

Alexis Calder writes sassy heroines and sexy heroes with a sprinkle of sarcasm. She lives in the Rockies and drinks far too much coffee and just the right amount of wine.

# Also by Alexis Calder

Rejected Fate Series

Darkest Mate

Forbidden Sin

Feral Queen


Moon Cursed Series

Wolf Marked

Wolf Untamed

Wolf Chosen


Royal Mates Series

Shifter Claimed

Shifter Fated

Shifter Rising


Academy of Elites Series

Academy of Elites: Untamed Magic

Academy of Elites: Broken Magic

Academy of Elites: Fated Magic

Academy of Elites: Unbound Magic


Brimstone Academy Series

Brimstone Academy: Semester One

Brimstone Academy: Semester Two

Romcom books published under Lexi Calder:

In Hate With My Boss

Love to Hate You

Made in the USA
Monee, IL
12 June 2022

97910493R00166